CHICKEN LITTLE WAS RIGHT

CHICKEN LITTLE WAS RIGHT

JEAN RURYK

ST. MARTIN'S PRESS   NEW YORK

To my daughter, Jenny

Design by Basha Zapatka

Library of Congress Cataloging-in-Publication Data

Ruryk, Jean.
    Chicken little was right / Jean Ruryk.
        p.   cm.
    "A Thomas Dunne book."
    ISBN 0-312-10952-0 (cover)
    1. Middle aged women—Fiction.   2. Mothers and daughters—Fiction.   3. Bank robberies—Fiction.   4. Hostages—Fiction.
    I. Title.
    PR9199.3.R79C48   1994
    813'.54—dc20   94-1119
                                                            CIP

First Edition: July 1994
10 9 8 7 6 5 4 3 2 1

1

Six days ago, I was on the rear patio stripping ninety-year-old varnish from a Victorian piecrust table.

The sun was beaming down on a rain-washed June world. A mourning dove lamented from the depths of a flowering plum tree and life was just fine. Restoring period furniture for antique dealers paid for the essentials and there was no foreseeable problem I couldn't resolve in twenty minutes.

Six days ago, bank robbery, burglary and bombs were the stuff of television cop shows and Donald Westlake novels.

Then the phone rang.

I peeled off the rubber gloves, checked the soles of my shoes for stripper muck, raced to the kitchen and snatched up the phone on the fourth ring.

"Hello?"

"I have a collect call for Catherine Wilde from Mrs. Daisy Powell," the phone operator droned in my ear. "Do you accept the charges?"

I felt a twinge of alarm. Daisy, my daughter's mother-in-law, doesn't like me enough to call for a long-distance chat. Not even collect.

She had been a British war bride, a cockney who had successfully resisted assimilation by the colonials. We'd got off on the wrong foot from the start. I'd told her the Staffordshire dogs she had were not only not Staffordshire, but were reproductions less than fifty years old. I should have known better. But she had asked and I'd assumed she wanted to know. She'd had them appraised, found I was right and never forgiven me. We'd never surmounted that original antipathy. Neither of us had tried.

"I'll accept the charges."

"Go ahead, caller," I heard the operator say, then Daisy's nasal voice came over the wire.

"Hello, Catherine. It's Daisy."

"Hi, Daisy. How are you?" A mistake. There are two topics on which Daisy can expound endlessly: the British monarchy and the state of her health.

"Well, not too well, really. My blood pressure is up to one-fifty over a hundred, and my doctor—"

"Daisy," I interrupted before she got into full stride. "You didn't call to bring me up to date on your blood pressure. What is it? What's happened?"

"I really don't know quite how to tell—"

"Daisy. Try one-syllable words."

Dead silence.

I capitulated. "I'm sorry, Daisy. Is something wrong?"

"Well. Yes." She sounded mollified. "Actually . . . well . . . there's been an accident."

"An accident? Laurie?"

"Well. Actually, Laurie and Andy. They were on their way to work. It seems a lorry went out of control. Or was it a bus? No. I'm sure they said—"

"How bad?"

"How bad?" she echoed.

I gritted my teeth. "Are they hurt?"

"Oh. I think so. But I just got here. I had to find a cab. You'd think Mort could have—"

"Which hospital?"

"Hospital? Oh. Saint Paul's, I think. Isn't Saint Paul's the one with the—"

"I'll be there in five hours." I hung up.

I moved everything from the patio into the basement. I called Canterbury House Antiques and told Charlie delivery of his tables would be delayed. I showered hastily, threw some clothes into a suitcase and the suitcase into the car. I explained to Brandy why she had to be left at a kennel. She did not take it well.

The four-hundred-mile drive was white-knuckle all the way. Each time I forced myself to slow down to the legal limit, dread made me lead-footed again. Approaching the city, I found myself trapped in rush-hour traffic, wedged firmly in the center lane. I watched my exit lane flash by. Two exits too far, palms sweating on the steering wheel, I made it off the expressway.

Threading back through unfamiliar streets, I lost all sense of direction and drove in circles until I stumbled on St. Paul's. I abandoned my car in the hospital parking lot and raced up the marble steps, into the coolness of the hushed lobby.

At the information desk, a gray-haired woman directed me to the eighth floor. I hurried to the elevator bank and waited. The grave faces around me, the muted voices, the discreet *pong*ing of a call bell, all increased my sense of urgency.

The elevator stopped at every floor in its ponderous ascent. An ashen-faced old man with a walker inched his way in on two. An empty gurney was wheeled in on three, off on four. Patients in slippers and dressing gowns crept in and out, orderlies pushing carts came and went. At the eighth floor, rigid with frustration and a growing sense of foreboding, I escaped.

I rounded the corner from the elevators and there they were.

Daisy in her flowered Liberty-print dress, white gloves and the rigid curls she believes emphasize a remote resemblance to Queen Elizabeth. Caroline, her daughter, so cowed by mother and marriage as to be almost invisible. And Caroline's husband, Mort.

Mort is a thickset man, broad-chested, with powerful arms and a torso too long for his short legs. His head is leonine, a dun-colored mane radiating from a fleshy face. Deep lines bracket his full lips, heavy brows shadow his pale amber eyes. He's a man of tics and twitches, constantly tugging at his brows and jowls with stubby, tobacco-stained fingers. He wears an aura of rage, of violence held barely under control.

Nobody ever calls him Morty. Not even Caroline.

As I approached, the doors behind him swung open and a young doctor dressed in creased pale-green coveralls emerged, his face weary, his step purposeful.

"Mrs. Powell," he addressed Daisy gently, "I'm so sorry. We couldn't help your son. We did everything we could. There was just too much damage."

Daisy stared at him, uncomprehending.

I reached out and touched his wrist.

"Laurie? My daughter?"

"You're Mrs. Powell's mother?" He rubbed his cheek, not meeting my eyes. "I'm sorry, Mrs. . . ."

"Wilde."

"Mrs. Wilde. We lost your daughter two hours ago."

For the next two days, I was in the benumbed state that shields us briefly from disaster and death. The world shrinks to a single dimension, a place peopled by remote, shadowy phantoms, a world of monochromatic color, muffled sound.

I stayed in Laurie's house, slept in her bed, brewed coffee and tea with supplies she had stocked. I sat in her quiet kitchen until the silence became a living presence, then deliberately smashed my coffee cup on the tiled floor. It didn't help.

I chose a casket for Laurie. I selected the dress in which she would be buried. I sat at the funeral home, hearing but not comprehending words of condolence from people I didn't know. And on the fourth day, I stumbled through the barbaric rituals of funeral and interment.

On the fifth day, I was jolted back into the real world.

2

$\mathcal{W}$e sat in the lawyer's office. Daisy, Caroline, Mort and I, listening to the terms of Laurie's will. It was short and to the point. Andy was her sole heir.

"Now. To proceed." The lawyer—Simpson? Simpkins?—cleared his throat, adjusted his Ben Franklin glasses and steepled his fingers.

"Andrew Duff Powell," he intoned. "The only will extant is dated fifteen years ago." He peered over his glasses. "The sole legatee is his sister, Caroline Anne Powell."

Mort leaned forward.

"My wife gets it all?" Mort has a deep voice. He speaks as though his words are released under pressure. In the quiet office, he sounded coarse and loud.

Simpson-Simpkins nodded.

"Laurie Wilde Powell predeceased her husband. Andrew Duff Powell inherited her estate. Upon the death of Andrew Powell, Caroline Powell Snyder became heir to their combined estates."

"Hold on," Mort intervened. "We get the house?"

"The house is included in the estate. Yes."

"*Just a minute!*"

The first crack had appeared in the glass surrounding me. I glanced at Mort. He sat with thick knees spread, hands clasped over the beginning of a paunch that strained at the buttons of his charcoal-colored corduroy jacket. Beside him was pale Caroline, her gaze fixed on her shoes. She felt my eyes on her. She didn't look up, but her cheeks flushed.

"The house is going to have to be put up for sale," I said.

"Like hell it is," Mort snapped. "The house is mine, lady."

I looked at Daisy, who quickly dropped her eyes. I turned to Simpson-whatever.

"About a year ago, Laurie phoned me," I said, forcing back the anger welling in my throat. "She and Andy had the opportunity to purchase a house, in a good neighborhood, for less than it was worth. It was in a state of disrepair. Their idea was to live in the house for two years, renovate and redecorate, then sell it for twice what they paid."

I glanced at Daisy. She had been aware of the arrangement. She glared back at me, tight-lipped.

"They asked me to lend them the money they needed," I continued. "The agreement was that they make monthly payments—equal to the interest my money would have earned—until the house was sold. At which time, they would repay what they had borrowed."

The lawyer studied me over the rims of his glasses. "And you did this?" he asked.

I nodded. "I cashed in my savings."

"How much was involved?"

"Sixty thousand dollars. All I had."

"You have documentation?"

"Documentation?"

"You need a document stating clearly that the sixty thousand dollars was a loan—*not a gift*—made by you to your daughter. A loan that was to be repaid upon sale of the house. A legal paper signed by your daughter, her husband and by you. Witnessed, preferably." He removed his glasses, tapped the papers on his desk with them. "Documentation."

"This was my daughter. I didn't need documentation."

"You need it now, Mrs. Wilde," he said dryly.

I stared at him silently as his meaning sank in.

"Okay. I want to understand this," I said carefully. "Are you saying I can't claim the money I lent them?"

Simpson-Simpkins nodded. "Precisely."

I looked at Mort and remembered his avid face at the news of Andy's death. He had known then that Laurie had been the first to go. There was triumph now, and malice, in his narrowed gaze.

"There's one other little item," he said. "Laurie owned half the house you live in. It's mine. And I'm claiming it."

A flash of sheer outrage stung me to my feet. "*Over my dead body!*" I hissed at him.

I was halfway across the reception room when I heard him call after me.

"That's okay with me, lady," he shouted. "And the sooner, the better."

3

$\mathcal{I}$ took the elevator down one flight and walked the corridor until I found a covey of lawyers. Eight names were lettered in gold on the heavy plate-glass door.

The receptionist glanced up briefly as I approached, then returned her gaze to her computer screen and continued typing. I studied her as I waited for her to acknowledge my presence.

Young. Twenty maybe? Oversized, tinted glasses. Creamy skin, oval face framed in a frizzy halo of hair streaked seven shades of blond. A petulant mouth, short upper lip, pouty lower.

The mouth tightened. She raised her eyes and lifted her brows at me. Her fingers remained on the keys.

"I'm sorry to interrupt you," I apologized. "These are law offices?"

"That's right." She made no effort to hide her impatience.

"I need to speak to a lawyer."

"Not without an appointment." She turned her attention back to the monitor screen.

I leaned forward.

"Look, miss," I said evenly. "I am aware that an appointment is ordinarily required. But it is essential I speak to a lawyer. There are eight lawyers listed on that door. It's entirely possible one of them may have three minutes to spare. Would you be kind enough to try. Please."

She ignored me and began typing, using the flat pads of her fingers on the keys to protect stiletto nails.

I felt my cheeks flush at the calculated insolence. I reached over and pressed the shift key on her computer keyboard. Her hands flew away as though the board had scorched her fingers.

"Listen to me, girlie." I bent across the desk. With my face inches from hers, I stretched my eyelids in an unfocused glare and bared my teeth. I dropped my voice to a guttural growl. "Get yourself on that phone . . . now . . . and find out if one of those eight lawyers will see me. Otherwise, and you can trust me on this, I am going to beam you off the face of this planet."

She reared back in her chair, pressing as far from me as she could, and reached hastily for the phone. With wide eyes fastened on my face, she punched a button in the base.

"Mr. Vineberg? There's a . . . a *person* here who would like to see a . . . see you." She bit her lip. "No. No appointment." She listened, then said shakily, "I'm sorry, Mr. Vineberg. Please come out here. Please!"

She replaced the receiver. "He . . . he'll be right out."

"Thank you." I smiled at her. It made her more uneasy. She watched me with the narrow concentration a mouse gives the cat stalking it.

A heavy teak door behind her flew open, pushed forcefully from within by a short, plump man in a pink shirt. He burst into the reception area, eyes glinting behind heavy-rimmed glasses.

He looked at me. He looked behind me. He looked at the receptionist. With an almost perceptible mental shrug, he turned his attention back to me.

"You wanted to see me?" His voice was pleasantly deep and masculine, his tone wary.

I nodded. "Three minutes." I held up three fingers. "All I need is three minutes of your time."

"Are you selling something?"

"Selling? No. No, I need advice. I won't take more than three minutes."

He studied me, then gestured me in. I followed him down a lushly carpeted hall to an open office door. He stepped aside to let me pass, followed me in and closed the door.

Circling the laden desk, he indicated the chair opposite. When I was seated, he sat down, folded his arms across his chest and eyed me dispassionately.

I pointed to the ceiling. "I've just come from a Mr. Simpson upstairs—" I began.

"Upstairs?"

"A lawyer. He's up—"

"Simpkins. Simpkins, Waterson and Pauley."

Simpson. Simpkins. What did it matter? I knew I wouldn't remember. I launched into my narrative, starting with the loan to Laurie and Andy, ending with Mort's taunting insult.

He glanced at his watch.

"Two minutes, ten seconds. You rehearse on your way down?"

There was no hint of sarcasm in his tone. I decided to take the question literally.

"I used to produce radio and television commercials. There's a stopwatch built in up here." I tapped my temple. "And I think we've just wasted fifteen of my last twenty seconds."

He checked his watch. His eyebrows lifted.

"Almost to the second," he said. Then his face relaxed in a smile. He leaned across the desk, extending his hand.

"Saul Vineberg, Mrs. . . ."

"Wilde. Catherine Wilde."

I put my hand in his and we appraised one another.

He was in his mid to late forties. He had intelligent eyes, a deep warm brown under heavy black brows. His scalp was naked and tanned above a narrow fringe of graying black hair. I've always suspected that men who grow long side hair and comb it across a bald pate have an infinite capacity for self-deception. Saul Vineberg wasn't kidding himself.

He released my hand and leaned back in his chair.

"Okay, Mrs. Wilde," he said pleasantly. "May I call you Catherine?" I nodded and he continued. "Great. I'm Saul. And now that we're friends, would you please tell me what a nice lady like you did to scare the pants off Debbie?"

"Debbie? The receptionist?"

"Our resident airhead. What the hell did you say to her?"

"I told her I might get rude."

"Debbie?" He eyed me askance. "Debbie says please for the first time in her life because you might get rude?"

"Maybe it's the way I said it."

"Hah." Saul snorted.

"Hah," I said. "When my daughter was five, she informed me she believed in God because she'd seen him on television."

Saul frowned. "You lost me. How does that apply?"

"It applies," I assured him. "Look. Debbie's generation grew up in front of a TV set. They've watched a world where anything is possible. They've seen Satan's yellow eyes born in the face of a child. They've seen invaders from alien worlds, lizards taking on human form and moving in next door. Little old ladies who turn out to be intergalactic witches. Maybe they don't believe. But they don't entirely, one hundred percent, disbelieve either."

Saul nodded, amused. "So? Are you?"

"Are I what?"

"An intergalactic witch." He grinned. "Just checking."

"I wish. I'd zotz Mort." I leaned forward. "Can he really do it to me? Mort?"

Saul sobered instantly.

"I'm sorry, Catherine." There was genuine regret in his voice. "He really can. Number one." He held up his hand

12

and ticked off his index finger. "You can forget your sixty thousand. From what you tell me, you have zilch to prove you gave them the money."

I nodded.

Saul grimaced. "Catherine, pardon me. But that wasn't too bright." He tapped his middle finger. "Number two. Your daughter was half-owner of your house."

"I . . ." My throat closed painfully and I blinked back sudden tears. Not now. Not here. I could not, *would not*, cry now. "I didn't expect to outlive my child."

Saul glanced away tactfully. "No parent does."

"But." He turned back to me. "Your daughter left her estate to her husband. Who probably procrastinated the hell out of making a new will. Most people do. So his estate went to his sister. Who, from what you tell me, is a cipher. Which leaves us with Mort. So you're going to have to deal with Mort. And Mort, unfortunately, can force you to pay him half the evaluated cost of your house if he so chooses."

"I can't pay him anything. He's got it all."

Saul shook his head. "Not yet he ain't. He can force you to sell if you don't pay."

My heart sank. "Can he really do that?"

"Trust me, Catherine. He can really do that." Saul frowned, pulling at his lower lip. "Would groveling work with Mort?"

"Groveling? Like *please, Mort, don't do this to me?*"

"Along that line. Yes."

I shook my head.

"The first time I met Mort, I was visiting Laurie and Andy. They had a compact disc player. I was very impressed. Next day, Mort phoned and told me he could get me one at a good discount. He delivered. I paid. And when Andy came home, he told me the damn thing probably fell off the back of a truck."

Saul's brows lifted. "Hot?"

"Scalding." I shrugged. "I demanded my money back. I probably got a bit sanctimonious about it. Anyway, Mort is not fond of me."

"Uh-huh," Saul grunted, then looked thoughtful. "Is that what he does for a living? Flog hot merchandise?"

"Actually, he has a fleet of taxis. Four or five, I think. Does four or five count as a fleet?"

"Four, fifty, whatever." He dismissed the taxis with a wave of his hand. "So. Outside of grabbing everything he can get, Mort is probably working off a personal grudge."

"And it's legal?"

"It's legal." Saul grimaced, shook his head. "I'm sorry as hell, Catherine. What can I tell you?"

"You've told me what I need to know and you've been more than generous with your time." I reached for my handbag. "Now, if you'll tell me what I owe you, I'll get out and let you get back to work."

"Forget it. You don't owe me anything."

I glanced up at him in surprise.

"What the hell, Catherine. You're being screwed enough. Let me make you my *mitzvah*, my good deed for the day." He grinned and I had a sudden glimpse of how he must have looked as a boy. "Hey, the look on Debbie's face was worth more than I could honestly charge you anyway."

I started to protest, then realized he was sincere.

"Thank you, Saul."

He waved a deprecatory hand. "What are you going to do?"

"Do? Probably rob a bank," I was startled to hear myself say.

I was born in October of twenty-nine, the month and year that launched the dirty thirties. Two memories epitomize the Great Depression years of my childhood—my father's gesture of pulling empty pockets inside out, and his despairing solution to the way things were. *Rob a bank.*

"Rob a bank?" Saul echoed. "With your luck? Take my advice. Also for free. Don't do it."

I rose to my feet and extended my hand.

"Thank you, Saul. For your time. For your *mitzvah*. For your advice."

"What advice?" He rose, took my hand in his. "Don't rob a bank? I'm only sorry I couldn't be of more help. Unless you can find a receipt—"

"Which I don't have."

"Or your son-in-law made out a later will—"

"Which he doesn't seem to have done."

"—it appears you're up the proverbial creek."

"And my house? Mort?"

"What can I tell you? Wait and see what he does. He has your daughter's house. He has any other assets there might be in the estate. Maybe he won't go after your house."

"But don't count on it."

"I wouldn't." He spread his hands, shrugged. "When it comes to money, guys a hell of a lot nicer than Mort turn out to be real shitheels."

"Well . . ." I was suddenly too depressed to continue. "Thank you, Saul. At least I've had the pleasure of meeting you."

"The pleasure was mine. Good luck, Catherine."

I drove straight to Laurie's house.

I packed three cartons with her personal belongings, family photos and her paintings. I walked through the house for the last time, seeing it through a blur of tears.

By noon, I was on the road home.

Brandy was frantic with joy when I picked her up at the kennel. Once inside the car, she decided to punish me for having abandoned her. She sat erect on the rear seat, head averted, watching the streets roll by. When I reached back to pat her, she gave me a look of utter disdain and relented only when I turned into the driveway of home. With a tongue-lolling grin, she leaped from the car and raced to the front door of the house.

I was pulling my suitcase from the car trunk when I heard her growl. I looked up in astonishment.

Brandy, besides being the sweetest dog ever whelped, is an abject coward. She rarely barks, never growls. She handles unfriendly confrontations by positioning herself behind me and waving her tail.

Her rumbling growl continued, louder now. Her ears were laid flat, her tail tucked under. A ridge of stiffened hair bristled along her spine.

I could see nothing to alarm her. The house appeared the same as when I'd left. Still, I pushed my suitcase back into the trunk and approached with a distinct sense of unease.

The smell hit me when I opened the glass storm door. When I threw the inner door open, the stench was overpowering.

I pulled a tissue from my pocket, held it over my nose, swallowed hard and stepped into the foyer. Brandy followed, whining unhappily.

Spray-painted on the hall mirror, in red letters a foot high, were the words "Fuck You."

4

"Kids," the burly policeman said sourly. He rubbed his chest. "Think you can find some bicarb in this mess?"

The two officers had arrived within twenty minutes.

"Quinn," the larger man identified himself. He was fat and untidy, with the weary face and bilious eyes of a disenchanted basset hound. "This is Officer Krantz."

He indicated his tanned, trim, sandy-haired partner. Krantz muttered *"Jesus Christ"* at the stench in the house. It was his first and last comment.

They followed me from room to room, Quinn plodding, Krantz tagging behind, carefully shunning the walls as though contact would soil his starched blue shirt.

My bedroom had been thoroughly trashed, every drawer pulled out and overturned, the closet gutted. Clothes, shoes, handbags and boxes were strewn over the floor. Perfume bottles lay smashed. The bedside lamp shades had been slashed, the bed pulled apart. The curtains were tied in tight knots.

And "Fucking Cunt" had been scrawled in lipstick across the dresser mirror.

In the bathroom, the toilet bowl was clogged with bottles and boxes from the medicine chest. The shower curtain, towels and the floor mat floated in the bathtub. And written in soap on the mirror was the word "Motherfucker."

Laurie's former bedroom fared only slightly better. Her braided rug was awash with papers. Cartons of old report cards, class photos, notebooks from her school days and her early drawings had been upended and dumped.

Her mirror had been spared the lurid graffiti.

"Punks used up their entire vocabulary," Quinn grunted.

The living room was a shambles, the basement a disaster. But it was the kitchen that brought me close to tears of anger and self-pity.

Centered on the floor was an obscene mess of broken eggs, soured milk, broken pickle and mayonnaise jars, lettuce wilted brown, blackened fish, meat glistening with a rainbow sheen of slime, rotting peaches alive with fruit flies, and a pale brown something growing green mold.

A heavy dusting of flour lay on the counters and on the appliances. Sugar crunched underfoot. There was syrup in the cutlery drawer, molasses in the linen drawer, liquid soap in the spice drawer.

My cookbooks, swollen to twice their bulk, lay submerged in the scummy water of the stopped-up sink. I plunged my hand in, yanked the plug and turned on the cold-water tap.

The bicarbonate of soda had been spared. I prepared a glass for Quinn. He drank it down, grimaced, thumped his chest and belched loudly behind a meaty hand.

"Heartburn," he growled. "Sorry."

I waved aside his apology. "You said kids. You really think kids did this?"

He nodded, stifling a second rolling belch.

"But why? Why would they do this to me? To somebody they don't even know? Why didn't they just take the TV set and the stereo and go?"

"You missing any money? They get any cash?"

"No. I took what cash I had with me."

"Jewelry? Liquor?"

"I don't have any."

"Had to be kids. That's what they're after. They didn't

get any. So this—" he included the entire house with a wide sweep of his arm "—is what you might call their way of expressing their displeasure."

Krantz, standing detached in the doorway, snorted.

Quinn ignored him.

"Look, Mrs. Wilde," he said kindly. "You got a shovel and a couple garbage bags, I'll give you a hand getting all this crap up off the floor. Least get rid of some of the stink."

I held the bags. Quinn shoveled, grunting. Krantz stood aloof, feet planted wide, arms akimbo, an expression of distaste on his face.

They departed, Krantz heading for the patrol car, Quinn lingering to assure me he'd be in touch if anything turned up.

". . . but don't hold your breath. This could have been any of a bunch of kids we got our eye on, and even if we nail the right ones, they're juveniles. They show up in court, they give us the finger. They walk away laughing. So nobody's going to bust his ass, you see what I mean. Sorry. But that's how it goes." He shrugged his disgust for the way things were and shambled off to the patrol car.

I turned back to my ravaged house.

Don't think about it. Just do it.

I slapped the Soviet Army Chorus on the turntable, turned the volume up to thunderous and attacked the kitchen.

Two hours later, the worst was over and Brandy consented to come in from the rear patio. I fed her, opened a can of beans for myself and ate them cold, leaning against the sink. My anger was giving way to depression. I knew that if I sat down, I might never get up again.

It was past midnight when I finished in the bathroom. I was too exhausted to do more than put fresh linen on the bed. I crawled, aching and groaning, between the sheets.

5

$\mathcal{I}$'m not sure whether it was the sound of the doorbell that dragged me up out of sleep or if it was Brandy pressing a cold, wet nose in my face.

A Federal Express van idled at the curb. The driver thrust a clipboard under my nose. I signed and he trotted off, muttering *'have a good day'* like a curse, leaving me staring bleary-eyed at the embossed return address on a pale gray envelope.

Simpkins, Waterson & Pauley.

More than anything, I wanted coffee and a cigarette, and neither was available. I threw on some clothing, splashed cold water on my face, bundled Brandy into the car and drove to the nearest shopping mall.

Purchasing a pack of cigarettes, the first in two years, I ordered an elaborate breakfast and ate, doggedly ignoring the gray envelope in my handbag. Finally, with a second cup of coffee and a fourth cigarette, I tore it open.

I read the letter three times before I was able to fully absorb its import.

Mort was demanding thirty-five thousand dollars for his share of my house. Payment within sixty days. He would "otherwise press for sale of the property at full current market value, of which the proceeds of said sale would constitute a greater sum in which he was legally entitled to share equally. Would I please notify the undersigned . . ."

So much for have a good day.

6

I sat on the rear patio watching the dying sun set fire to the undersides of a skim of low-riding clouds. The mourning dove in the plum tree, in deadly earnest now, wept for his lost love, *oh woe, woe, woe.*

Six days ago, I had been at work on this same patio, blissfully certain the universe was unfolding as it should.

The pieces of furniture I had stripped that day were in the basement, caked with the scum of two fire extinguishers the punks had found and emptied, spraying with vicious abandon.

All my junk—tools, trays of nails and screws, period fabrics garnered over the years, antique porcelain hardware, beveled mirrors, hand-carved wood trims, several fine hand-painted panels—all were encrusted with dried gray foam. A few days of scouring might put me back in business, but even if I worked day and night, I could never meet Mort's demands.

My chances of obtaining a bank loan were *"very dubious,"* according to the politely patient bank manager. Remortgaging the house was *"quite seriously out of the question,"* said the equally patient trust officer over the phone. Other than the house, I possess no assets. I have no pension. I am not employed. And I am sixty years old.

Forty years ago, an aging, disenchanted newspaper writer, in an alcoholic mixture of allegories, summarized for me what life is all about.

"Get past puberty, kid," he intoned, owlishly drunk, "it's just a fucking series of pratfalls. Every time you think this is it, I'm rolling, they yank the fucking rug out from under you. So you get up off your goddamn ass. One more time. Start climbing that fucking mountain one more time. And one day you get a grip up on top, up where the sun always shines, and they stomp on your fingers and you're back on your goddamn ass, fucked by the fickle finger of fate." He released a beery belch. "Circumstances beyond your control."

"What circumstances?" Probably I was goading him. I was twenty. Everything was ahead for me. I truly believed I was master of my fate and I judged failure harshly.

He turned reddened, angry eyes on me.

"Circumstances, for Christ's sake. Asshole politics. Power. War. People. Fucking rotten people. Fucking rotten world."

"Who's *they?*"

"Wha?"

"*They* stomped on your fingers. They. Who's they?" Twenty-year-old smartass.

"*They. Them.* The gods. The fucking gods. Sitting on their fucking cloud laughing their fucking heads off watching us get up off our goddamn ass one more time always one more time until you can't get up one more time and you fucking well die."

I hadn't particularly liked him. I had thought him cynical and sour. Now, forty years later, remembering, I found myself wondering.

So how many falls for me?

Marriage, the first and most painful fall of all. Too many years of frantic effort to prop up a facade of normalcy, of fending off bailiffs, of lies piled on lies, before I admitted to myself what departed friends had learned far sooner. That the charming, convivial man I thought I had married was a liar, a deadbeat and a fucking drunk.

I walked away. No. I ran away with five-year-old Laurie,

leaving behind what little was left in a house about to be repossessed, and went back to the advertising agency where I had worked before Laurie was born.

For four years, I produced government television and radio commercials and training and tourism films. And, finally, promos for an election. The opposition coasted in on a landslide. The new mandarins chose a new agency and sixteen of us were out on the street.

With no job on the horizon and with my savings draining, I began pounding the pavement. I picked up assignments here and there from smaller agencies, a television station, a production house. After two years of dodging the landlord, eating a lot of pasta, buying clothes at church bazaars, I began to make a good living as a freelance producer.

The ten years that followed were the good years. I had all the work I could handle and I had Laurie. Those were the Helen Reddy *You and Me Against the World* years. I wonder how many single mothers with an only child adopted that song as their own?

Then the gods stepped on my fingers. A drunken driver careened through a red light into the studio location van in which I was a passenger and I woke up in the hospital with a broken shoulder, three broken ribs and a broken hip.

Somewhere I read, or heard, the statistic contending that most families are only two pay checks away from the streets. I believe it. By the time I was discharged from the hospital, Laurie had been forced to leave college and find a job. To pay the three months' penalty clause permitting us to vacate our apartment, I sold off the antiques I had collected and moved to a smaller place.

We lived on Laurie's waitress wages while the insurance company dithered and delayed. I learned to walk again. And I learned I was finished as a freelance. Most of the people I had worked with had connected with new producers. Some had moved on or retired, and the young hot-shots who replaced them were disdainful of anyone over thirty.

The insurance company finally settled and I found the house I wanted.

It was old. It was in wretched condition. But the building was sound, located in a pleasant suburb. And the price was low. The owner, a cheerfully garrulous old woman pushing ninety, had married into it at twenty. Widowed, she had given up any pretense of maintenance. Or of housekeeping.

For fifty years, she had inherited the worldly goods of the multitude of relatives she had outlived. From attic to basement, the house was crammed with furniture, pictures, books, bibelots and junk, ranging from the era of Art Nouveau through Art Deco to postwar to the age of plastics. Up on blocks in the detached garage was a 1935 LaSalle coupe, complete with rumble seat. And everything, all of it, went with the house.

I held my breath until the deed was signed, sealed and delivered.

Selling the LaSalle paid for renovations on the antiquated plumbing and wiring systems. A portfolio of hand-colored Audubon lithographs, two large cartons of old Christmas-tree decorations and a drawerful of valentines, postcards and photographs, some dating to the turn of the century, covered the cost of appliances and a new furnace. The sale of two magnificent Pairpoint Puffy lamps, a gilt carriage clock and a frosted Lalique eagle's head car-hood ornament provided for a new roof.

We moved into a shambles, but neither of us cared. Laurie returned to school and I began sorting through the hoardings of five generations of pack rats.

For a year, I set up at flea markets every weekend, selling off the minor collectibles and the junk. It took another year to restore and dispose of the furniture, piece by piece, to the antique dealers, who had snapped up the Flow Blue dinnerware and the Carnival Glass, the Stevengraphs and the cast-iron toys. When one dealer, then another and another, gave me items out of stock to refinish, I had a new floor laid in the basement for a workshop, invested in good tools and took a course in upholstery basics.

Suddenly, at fifty-eight, I realized I had made it to that newspaperman's plateau, that place where the sun always shines. A hobby had become a means of livelihood and I was doing work I enjoyed. Laurie was married and happy with Andy, who was, in spite of his mother, one of the nicest men I'd ever met. I had money in the bank. I had a dog who was more intelligent and certainly more companionable than most people I had known. And I had a house I loved.

A house I was about to lose.

I stood up abruptly. Brandy, dozing at my feet, sprang away in alarm. She fell in at my heels as I walked past a stand of peonies, heavy with pink bloom, then loped off in pursuit of a bright orange butterfly.

At the high cedar hedge marking the rear property line, I stopped and looked back at the house.

A Hansel-and-Gretel house, Laurie had called it. The original house was small, built of stone, with leaded-glass casement windows. Two bedrooms had been tacked on sometime in the thirties, the exterior finished in white-washed stucco. A clapboard extension housing the kitchen had been a postwar addition. With three roof levels and no two windows the same, the place looked as if it had been built by tipsy elves. But overhead was the shelter of towering elms, and nestling close were lilac trees blooming mauve and deep purple and white. And ringing the property was a dense cedar hedge that hid me from my neighbors.

The rear patio, built by Laurie and Andy the year they were getting to know one another, was shaded on hot afternoons by an ancient oak tree that was a nesting place for birds and an easy escape route for the squirrels who teased Brandy unmercifully.

The house was worth less than the land on which it sat and would probably be bulldozed by developers when they began to rape the green and peaceful neighborhood. Selling now, I might realize what I had paid, but certainly not more. After paying off Mort and the mortgage, I might have enough left to rent a dreary room somewhere and live on dog food for the rest of my life.

Self-pity gave way to a surge of anger. Rage and hatred aimed at Mort. Resentment toward Andy for failing to rewrite his will. But mainly anger directed at myself.

There really is no fool like an old fool.

Suddenly, without warning, I was overcome by throat-tearing sobs. I slid down to the grass and wept. For Laurie, for Andy, for myself.

Brandy, frightened by sounds she had never heard from me, tried to crawl into my lap. I pushed her away. She persisted, thrusting her nose beneath my chin, licking tears. I twisted away, brought my knees up and leaned my elbows on them. She crawled, pushing her head up between my thighs, and whined softly. I brought my knees together, trapping her. She scrabbled backward. Free, she barked at me twice, indignantly, *What in hell did you do that for?*

I couldn't help laughing.

"Okay. Okay. It's over," I told her.

Her tail swept back and forth, then she sat, facing me, her head tilted, her ears erect, expression quizzical.

"I don't know what I'm going to do." I stroked her thick ruff. "If I sell the house, I'll have nowhere to work. If I don't sell, Mort'll yank it out from under me. I'm too old to get a decent job and too young to get an old-age pension. Like the man said, I'm fucked by the fickle finger of fate."

I stood up, brushed the grass from my legs and started back to the house. Brandy pranced ahead.

Halfway, I stopped. At that moment, for the first time,

I fully understood that I was going to lose everything. I was really going to lose it all. And there was nothing I could do about it. It occurred to me then that my father, through the Depression years, must have known this same helplessness and frustration. I groaned aloud, startling myself. I sounded the way he had so many years ago.

Brandy heard. She halted, puzzled.

"Hey," I called to her. "How'd you like to rob a bank?"

I was kidding. But later, lying in bed sleepless, the anger I've sublimated all my life as unproductive began to sear my brain.

We all start out so open, so eager. Avid for life, so sure we can be the golden ones if we try hard enough. And life slaps all our fresh young faces. Sometimes I watch the beautiful young families in grocery-store lineups and wonder in what way life is going to screw them and sour them and hang them out to swing in the wind.

Nobody ends up with the life they planned.

The ground has been cut out from under me twice in my life. I've lost everything twice, started over twice. Like a cat twisting in midair, I've landed on my feet and muddled on, licking my wounds.

But in those days, I was young. And there was Laurie. Now I'm going to lose it all again, and this time there's nothing I can do, nowhere I can turn to save myself.

So go rob a bank.

What the hell. At least go find out if it's possible.

7

$\mathcal{I}$n the morning, I went shopping for a bank.

I quickly discounted those contained in large, enclosed malls. Too many people strolling. Too many confusing passageways branching off in all directions. And too far to run.

After three hours of filling out deposit slips on nonexistent accounts in a series of banks in small neighborhood plazas, I found what seemed an ideal setup.

The plaza was L-shaped, with each store exiting into the parking lot. The base of the L was a food supermarket. Between the supermarket and the row of shops forming the vertical stem of the L was a walled passage leading to the rear of the plaza, where deliveries were made, and to the apartment buildings on the street beyond. The bank was one shop removed from the passage.

I filled out one more deposit slip at the marble-topped central counter and studied the place.

There were about a dozen customers waiting in line, most of them seniors, bespectacled and sensibly shod. A short, middle-aged woman with frizzy orange hair shifted impatiently from one stilt heel to the other, a canvas bag and a deposit book clutched to her remarkable bosom. A young mother kept a watchful eye on her child, a cherubic boy of three or four years whose chattering drew indulgent smiles from the bank personnel and the elderly lineup.

Through her open door, I could see the manager, a tall woman in her forties. The loans officer was a sallow, rather effeminate-looking young man. All the tellers were youthful women, with easy smiles. Three cameras. No guard, armed or otherwise. A small bank in a small shopping plaza in a quiet neighborhood.

It seemed the perfect where. What I needed was the how.

How does one person, alone, rob a bank? More to the point, how does one old—oldish—lady person, alone, rob a bank? Wave a gun and shout this is a stickup? The men in the white coats would arrive before the laughter died.

I studied the four fresh-faced young tellers.

What manner of threat would deter these four young women, girls actually, from activating the alarm buttons I was sure were less than a step away?

What would stop me from hitting the panic button?

If, protecting the bank's money, I was sure I would die? Or if, protecting the bank's money, one of the blue-haired ladies or balding men waiting patiently in line would die?

My eye fell on the little boy, propped up on the counter while the teller served his mother.

If a child should die?

If I believed, *if I knew*, this dewy-skinned, dimple-cheeked child would die before my eyes as a consequence of my action, would I sound an alarm?

Back in the car, I was about to turn the key in the ignition when a thought occurred. If the police patrolled the shopping center on a regular schedule, I could have a real problem.

I withdrew the key and opened the door. Brandy grumbled from the rear seat. She'd had enough of the car for the day. I told her I'd be right back and went into the shop beside the bank, a dry-cleaning establishment.

Behind the counter, an overweight woman with hair the color of straw looked up from the TV crossword puzzle she was working on and raised penciled eyebrows at me.

"My groceries!" I cried, pointing at the door. "Somebody stole my groceries!"

"What?" The plucked brows came down. "Whadyou say?"

"Someone stole my groceries! Out front. Someone stole my groceries right out of my car!"

"Yeah? No kidding. Was it locked?"

"I was only going to be a minute. I went into the bank. When I came out, they were gone! Somebody stole my groceries right out of my car!"

"Well, look. Hey." She shrugged plump shoulders. "You don't lock your car. I mean, hey."

"What about police? Aren't there police around here?"

"Police?" She snorted. "You kidding?"

"Don't the police patrol this place?"

"You gotta be kidding. Last time I seen a patrol car around here, the supermarket opened, they're giving away free coffee and doughnuts. That's three years ago." She gestured at the phone. "You wanna call the cops, go right ahead."

"Will they come? I mean, will they come right away? I was on my way to the dentist."

She shrugged again. "The video store down the way, it gets held up, they come half an hour after Gracie calls. You go ahead. You maybe could do better."

"Maybe I should go straight to the police station. Do you know where it is?"

"About two miles along." She thumbed to the right. "Can't miss it. Red brick building with this statue out front. Some godawful thing, you don't know what it's supposed to be." She dabbed the wetness at the corners of her mouth with thumb and index finger. "Believe me, you can't miss it."

"Maybe I should go there instead. Do you think I should? Maybe it would be faster. What do you think?"

"Suit yourself."

"Maybe I'll do that." I dithered a little longer. "Maybe

that's the best thing to do. Anyway, thanks for your trouble. You've been very nice."

"Yeah. Sure." Her eyes dropped back to her puzzle. She had forgotten me before I was out the door.

8

*T*oyLand had no guns anyone would mistake for the real thing. Even the water pistols were out of Star Wars. I bought the only toy that looked remotely lethal, a shiny plastic dagger.

After supper, on the patio watching the sun drop behind the cedars, I pondered on how to rob a bank without a gun.

An idea began to form. I discarded it as impracticable, but it continued to nudge at the corners of my mind. When no alternative suggested itself, I returned to the original idea and let it develop.

In the morning it still seemed like a good idea. Not a great idea, not inspired, just reasonably okay. I could pull it off alone. There was no danger of anyone being hurt.

And it might even work.

I went shopping.

At a Kmart across town, I found what I wanted: a printed cotton coat dress, with shiny metal buttons from collar to hem. The print, purple and orange daisies splashed on a green background, was unforgettable. The dress, wavering between classic shirtwaist and mock safari, had shoulder epaulets and five large pockets, including one on the right sleeve, all with more of the metal buttons tacked on.

I bought a gray wig. A large, yellow canvas tote bag. Pale beige support stockings. A pair of black oxford shoes with blocky low heels. And two rolls of self-stick, half-inch plastic tape, one white and one blue.

Back home, I dug up a pair of glasses with rhinestones set

in red plastic frames, and a pair of white cotton lace gloves, relics from the previous house owner.

I'm five-foot-six and weigh one hundred and twenty-five pounds. In the dress I looked chunkier, broader and thirty pounds heavier. The frizzed wig, the tacky glasses and a coating of pale face powder added years to my face. My legs and feet, encased in thick, dull hose and boxy, black shoes, belonged on a flatfooted bag lady. Or a man in drag.

Studying myself in the mirror, from the gray hair to the red glasses to the purple and orange and green print and the mustard-yellow bag, I decided I had achieved the effect I wanted.

Facing me in the mirror was somebody's decidedly color-blind, slightly ditzy grandmother.

Brandy opened one eye. Her eyelid had begun to droop back over the nictitating membrane when she sprang suddenly to her feet, ears erect. She approached me warily, sniffed at my ankles, then backed off and grumbled her annoyance at being momentarily hoodwinked. She turned her back on me and dropped to the floor, feigning sleep. In the mirror, I could see her watching as I changed into jeans and a sweatshirt.

When I left the bedroom, she followed on my heels. If we were playing games, she had no intention of being caught off base a second time.

The plastic dagger was six inches of shiny blade plus four of black haft molded to look like whipcord. It lay on the counter while I heated a darning needle over a candle flame. When the needle glowed red, I drilled a hole into the tip of the hollow blade. I sliced off the cap of the haft and filled the dagger with a couple of ounces of ketchup.

Holding the tip against my arm, I squeezed the haft. I got a handful of ketchup from the haft, but I also got a bright bead of ketchup on my arm from the tip of the blade.

I refilled the dagger, sealed the cap back on the haft with

Krazy Glue and tried again. The drop of ketchup on my arm looked like blood.

At nine-thirty the next morning, I was sitting in my car in the parking lot in front of the bank.

Brandy lay in the backseat snoozing fitfully. She was accustomed to waiting in the car while I shopped or ran errands. For me to remain in the car so long made her uneasy. As time passed, she changed position more frequently, sniffing my ear, nudging my shoulder, then flopping back, increasingly puzzled by my unusual behavior. Once she sat erect and I caught her studying me in the rearview mirror. When our eyes met, she said *whumpf* and dropped out of sight. I turned and looked at her.

"You're getting to be a real drag," I told her. "Where's your sense of adventure?"

She twitched her eyebrows at me.

By eleven o'clock, the dry-cleaning woman's assessment of police security had proved correct. There'd been no sign of a patrol car, neither on the street nor in the plaza. Traffic in and out of the parking lot was steady but not heavy, concentrated mainly near the food mart.

I went into the bank.

Watching the tellers, mentally blocking out the action much as I had done when planning a television commercial, I became aware of their routine. They did a lot of walking back and forth to a cage tucked in the corner where a woman sat behind a thick glass partition, accepting deposits and dispensing cash through a slot in the counter. Suddenly the lack of a security guard made sense. There was no cash at the tellers' stations. It was all in that bulletproof glass box.

Good or bad? I thought about it and decided it couldn't be better. I looked around, measured distances and knew I had it. The sequence, the timing.

I went back to the car and drove around the neighborhood. Eight blocks away, I found what I was looking for.

The parking lot of a small elementary school facing on a short, dead-end street. Six cars were parked against a windowless brick wall in an area laid out for ten. Across the road was a utility power station, surrounded by a high wire-mesh fence.

Back home, I went to work on my car license plate with a pair of scissors and the blue and white tapes. FNP 863 became EHR 308. For the balance of the afternoon, I experimented with makeup.

Thanks to my mother, my face is less wrinkled than sixty years says it should be. In addition to good bone structure and healthy skin, she passed on one sound word of advice: Drink ten glasses of water every day of your life. At fifty, I was able to pass myself off as forty. Given time to prepare and charitable light, I can probably still deduct ten years and get away with it.

Given a choice, I'd take wrinkles and a fat bank account.

Dark foundation under pale powder accentuated the crow's feet and the lines bracketing my mouth. Taupe eyeshadow leached out the blue in my eyes, leaving them a tired, rainy-day gray. I added a mole to my upper lip.

I was ready.

9

At ten-fifteen, there were eight customers in the bank. Three at the tellers' windows. Five in line. Two shopkeepers from the plaza, each carrying a canvas bag and deposit book. Three middle-aged women, a youthful couple in torn jeans and a sour-faced older man complaining aloud to nobody in particular about the closed fourth window.

I positioned myself just inside the door, glancing down at my watch every few moments as though waiting for someone. At ten-eighteen, the bank manager emerged from her office with her bag slung from her shoulder and left the bank. The loans officer ushered a heavy man in work clothes into his cubicle and shut the door.

Behind one teller's window, the teller was stamping and sorting papers, her plaque reversed to read "Closed." Two women, who looked like mother and daughter, paid bills at the second window. At the third, a thin old woman filled out a deposit slip with painful slowness. The fourth was closed.

An elderly couple shifted irritably, waiting in line. Behind them, a massive black woman, expression remote, stood stolidly patient.

At ten-nineteen, a young woman came in, holding her child by the hand. She crossed to the center island and placed her handbag on the marble surface, took a withdrawal slip and bent over it.

She was tall, five-eight or nine, lean and leggy in snug jeans. Tartan shirt knotted at the waist. Woven leather sandals. Large, scuffed saddlebag purse. Sun-streaked beige hair drawn tightly back, held by a tortoiseshell barrette. No jewelry. No makeup. Strong face with regular features, closer to classic than conventional prettiness.

Frowning, biting her lower lip, she looked distracted and tired, but not the type to dissolve into hysterics under stress.

Her daughter, somewhere between three and four years of age, wore a denim jump suit in a shade of blue matching her eyes. Her ponytail, tied with a blue ribbon, was a cascade of wheat-colored curls. She leaned against her mother's leg and eyed me solemnly.

I smiled. She turned her face away, then peeked back. I smiled again and withdrew a lollipop from one of the voluminous pockets of my hideous dress. She looked at it, up at me. I extended my hand, offering, smiling. She detached herself from her mother and took two hesitant steps.

"Cassie?" Her mother's head snapped around.

"May she have it?" I held up the lollipop.

"Oh. Well. I guess . . ." She frowned, abstracted. "Thank you. Say thank you, Cassie."

Cassie came to me, accepted the candy and said thank you with grave politeness.

"You're welcome, Cassie." I bent over her as she unwrapped the lollipop. "Do you watch TV, Cassie?"

She nodded, popped the candy in her mouth.

"Cops and robbers? Do you ever watch cops and robbers?"

She nodded.

"Would you like to play a game of cops and robbers with me? Just you and me? We can be the robbers."

She nodded, busy with her lollipop.

I took a deep breath. Exhaled.

Okay. Let's do it.

I snaked my right arm around her waist, lifted her and positioned her on my hip, holding her with her back pressed against me. I yanked the plastic dagger out of my pocket and placed the tip against her throat.

"*Freeze!*"

It was a voice I barely recognized, harsh and guttural, dredged up from the belly. I realized that until the moment I shouted the word, I hadn't known what I would say, hadn't given any thought as to how to get started. I'd been a producer, not a copywriter. But freeze?

Everyone froze. There was a moment of dead silence. Then Cassie, seeing the horror on her mother's face, wailed.

I squeezed the handle of the plastic knife. The concerted intake of breath meant the ketchup had beaded satisfactorily.

"One false move and I slit the kid's throat." *One false move. Had I really said* it?

Cassie whimpered. Her mother, wiping the fear from her face, reached out a trembling hand.

"It's all right, Cassie. You're all right. It's . . . it's a game. Keep very still. It's just a game."

I kicked the canvas bag toward her.

"You in the box!" I yelled. "She's going to bring the bag to you. Fill it. Do it fast. No alarms. I got nothing to lose. I even *think* I hear a siren, the kid dies."

Nothing moved. For a split second, I considered dropping Cassie and running. Then the black woman spoke up, her rich voice thinned.

"For God's sake! Do what the man says. Give him the money!" She glared at me, half in fear, half in righteous anger. "Mister, don't you hurt that child."

The freeze frame broke. Cassie's mother lunged for the bag, snatched it up and ran toward the waist-high partition separating the glass box from the main banking area. The gate was locked. She darted a wide look of sheer panic at me, then vaulted the barrier, long legs flashing.

Thirty-five seconds had passed.

The white-faced woman in the cage stuffed bank notes into the canvas bag held by Cassie's mother. The others were still. Silent. Staring.

The door to the loans manager's office remained shut. *Migod! He doesn't even know the place is being robbed.*

And Cassie was getting heavier by the second.

"Faster! You've got ten seconds. Or the kid dies. *You!*" I snarled at the terrified girl in the nearest window. "Open that gate. Now. *Move!*"

Cassie squirmed. I tightened my arm around her waist and positioned her more firmly on my hip. I could feel her draw a deep breath and I knew screams would follow. The game was lasting too long.

At least ninety seconds gone. I backed toward the door.

"Okay! That's it! Nobody move or the kid dies!"

I turned and made for the door, three long strides away. It swung wide as I approached and a man stood in the opening, blocking my way.

Liverlips.

The first thing I saw, those purple lips. A teacher in high school with the same mouth. Liverlips. Then the eyes, black and shiny, taking in every detail. I knew he could see through the disguise, would know me again, and I felt a *spang!* of pure panic. Then he stepped aside and I rushed past him, adrenaline spurting, intent only on getting away.

I made it to the passageway, running awkwardly, Cassie's legs flopping, striking at my shins. Behind me, I could hear the slap of sandals on cement and I knew Cassie's mother was on my heels. I risked a fast glance over my shoulder. She was carrying the canvas bag.

"What are you going to do?" Her voice was high and strained, breathless with fear, not effort. She ran easily, more than I could say for my lumbering trot. "Let Cassie go. I'll give you the bag. Let us go. I'll drop the bag right here. Just let me have Cassie."

"When we get to the car." I huffed out one word at a

time, not sure I would make it to the car. The passageway was twice as long as I remembered, Cassie six times as heavy as any three-year-old has a right to be. And she had begun to scream with fright.

Then I was out of the passageway, across the lane at the rear of the mall, across the street to where I had parked the car in front of the apartment buildings. I could see Brandy's face in the rear window and I concentrated on that as I staggered the last few steps.

"Okay." I turned, gasping for breath. "Drop the bag. Take her."

The bag hit the pavement. Cassie, sobbing, was pulled from my arms. A piercing scream stabbed into my ear.

Her ponytail was hopelessly entangled in the buttons of my phony safari dress. *There goes the ball game* and with that thought, panic vanished. I felt strangely calm and resigned.

I looked around, back at the passageway. No sign of pursuit, no activity in the lane. Yet.

"Give me Cassie," I ordered. "Take the bag and get into the passenger seat. You can untangle her hair while I drive." She started to protest. "Listen. I don't want anybody hurt. But I'm getting the hell out of here right now and I really don't want to yank the hair out of her head."

She hesitated, then handed Cassie to me. I struggled into the car, set Cassie astride the console between the bucket seats. By the time I'd dug the keys out of my pocket, her mother was in the passenger seat.

I turned the key. "Put the bag on the floor. Take Cassie in your lap," I instructed. "I'll try to lean your way so you can get her loose without hurting her too much."

With Cassie in her mother's lap, I was able to shift into drive. I pulled away from the curb.

At the cross street stop sign, I checked the traffic. Behind me, a black car with two men in the front seat. Halfway down the street to my left, a wide truck, followed by a green car and a bus. No sign of a police car.

I turned right. Two minutes later, I pulled into the parking lot of the elementary school. Seconds later, Cassie was free. She stopped crying and stared wide-eyed at Brandy.

"There's something I have to do," I said to her mother. "It won't take a minute. Then I'll drop you off. Don't try to run." I opened the car door, stepped out and spoke sternly to Brandy. "On guard!"

She sat up, ears erect, tongue drooping between sharp canine teeth. She looked menacing enough. They couldn't know she was laughing at me.

I scurried to the rear of the car and ripped the tape off my license plate. As I straightened, I caught movement from the corner of my eye.

A black car drifted slowly past the utility plant across the street. I felt a sudden chill. A black car had followed me from the street at the rear of the plaza.

The tinted windows of the car made it impossible to see the occupants. It glided slowly past, down to the dead end of the street. I rolled the tape into a sticky ball, shoved it into my pocket and hurried back into my car.

Cassie was leaning over her mother's shoulder, cooing at Brandy. Brandy was answering with soft *whuffs*, her tail sweeping ecstatically.

"Can I pat the doggie?" Cassie asked. "I want to pat the doggie, Mummy. Can I pat the doggie?"

"Her name is Brandy." With my eyes on the rearview mirror, I unbuttoned my dress to the waist. I slipped it off my shoulders and sat in a puddle of the hideous fabric.

The woman eyed Brandy. "What kind of dog is it?"

"Her mother was a collie." The black car made a U-turn. "Her father was a traveling salesman."

"BrandyBrandyBrandy," Cassie crooned. "I want to pat Brandy, Mummy. Can I?"

The black car rolled to a stop at the foot of the parking lot. Was it the same black car? I turned to Cassie's mother.

"You can put her in the backseat if you like."

"With the dog?" The woman's voice rose incredulously.

"She doesn't know she's a dog. She thinks she's Marilyn Monroe." The car crouched on the street like a black beetle. "Don't worry. She's a total wimp."

The woman lifted Cassie into the rear seat. Through the side mirror, I saw the black car start to roll, then speed away out of sight.

"*God damn you!*"

I turned to her, startled. Her eyes blazed blue sparks. Two crimson spots burned on her cheeks.

"You . . . you . . . monster!" Her voice shook with anger. "If I'd known that dog was a wimp, I'd . . . I'd have backed this goddamn car and smashed you into the ground. My God, what sort of woman are you? How could a woman . . . how could you . . . stick a knife into a baby's throat?"

I dug into the pocket where I had dropped the plastic knife, found it and passed it to her.

"Squeeze the handle."

The dagger point blurted red sauce onto her jeans.

"Ketchup," I said.

She made no effort to wipe the blob from her knee.

"You robbed a bank with this?" Stunned, she raised her eyes to mine. "A plastic toy full of ketchup?"

I handed her a Kleenex. "You were there."

"A plastic toy," she repeated, bewildered. "A plastic toy full of ketchup? Why not a gun, for God's sake? Why didn't you get a gun?"

"I don't know anything about guns. I wouldn't know where to get a gun and if I did, I wouldn't know how to load it. I'm afraid of guns." I shrugged. "I'd probably blow my foot off if I had one."

Suddenly she giggled, a mischievous, little-girl snicker.

Then she was laughing, lusty hoots of glee, impossible to resist. I began to laugh too, sheepishly, then uncontrollably. Relief from tension had us bursting out anew each time our glances met.

"If I'd known it was that easy," she gasped, "I'd have done it myself."

I wiped tears from my cheeks. She pointed to my feet. "The shoes," she squeaked. "Pure Mickey Mouse." And we were off again. I held my aching sides.

In the rearview mirror, I saw Cassie, her arms tight around Brandy's neck, her eyes round. She had heard her mother's anger and had picked up the edge of hysteria in our laughter.

"It's all right, Cassie," I assured her. "Grown-ups get silly sometimes. Are you all right?"

Her lower lip trembled. "I'm hungry, Mummy," she said in a small voice.

The mirth fled from her mother's eyes. She swiveled to face Cassie. "I know, honey. Soon. Okay?" She turned that blue gaze on me, her face set. "So what happens now?"

"I'm not sure. I hadn't planned on having company at this point." I glanced in the rearview mirror. The street was clear. "I can leave you here. I can drive you home. I can drop you off at a shopping mall. Whatever you want."

"Except back to the bank."

I nodded. "Except back to the bank. I'm sorry."

"You're sorry." Her tone was flat. "How nice. Look. I have no money. You dump us here, we'll just have to walk back to the bank. I don't have bus fare if you drop us at some mall. If you're so sorry, why don't you just take us back to where you found us?"

Her face wore an expression I knew from the inside. Eyes stretched wide to discourage tears. Lips held firm to belie their trembling.

"Mummy," Cassie whimpered from the rear seat. "Mummy? I'm hungry."

In spite of her tight control, a stricken look flashed in the woman's eyes. There was more to her distress than a hungry child.

"Has Cassie had breakfast?"

She looked away blindly, shook her head.

"You're in trouble, aren't you."

"Isn't everybody?" Her voice was rusty.

"What's your name?"

She looked back at me, startled. "Roxanne. Roxanne Parker."

"Okay, Roxanne." I started the car. "Let's do lunch."

10

"For someone who isn't really stupid, I guess I really am stupid." Roxanne smiled without humor.

We were in a distant mall, sitting at a round pink-metal table overlooking a supervised play pit. Cassie had eaten quickly and hungrily, her eyes on a sandbox where a teenage girl was teaching a gaggle of munchkins to build sand castles.

I had wiped off the makeup, locked the wig, the dress, the shoes and the canvas bag in the car trunk. Roxanne had studied me speculatively for the first few minutes, then relaxed, and we had chatted like normal ladies lunching with a child.

Her situation wasn't new or unusual, but I've never really believed there's comfort in knowing you're not the first or the only human being to suffer pain and humiliation. What hurts, hurts.

"How did you find out?"

She sipped her coffee, her gaze on Cassie playing happily below us in the sandbox. "Anonymous letter." She raised her eyes to mine, smiled a sour smile. "Short and to the point. 'Everybody but you knows your husband is screwing Dorothy Atkins.'"

"Someone you know?"

"I've met her. She owns the real-estate company Wayne works for. Wayne's an accountant."

"What did you do?"

"I left the letter on the kitchen table, took Cassie and went to a motel. I needed time to think."

"Did Wayne try to find you?"

"I don't think so. I waited a week. Then I drove back to the house. Nobody there. The locks changed. And a 'For Sale' sign stuck in the front lawn."

"You're kidding."

"So here I am. My car's sitting at the motel with an empty gas tank. I can't pay the motel bill. And I have a grand total of seven dollars and eleven cents left in the bank."

"Can he sell the house out from under you? Is it in his name?"

"The house belongs to his mother. If she says he can sell, he can sell."

"Can't you talk to her?"

"She lives in Florida somewhere. And that's one cold lady. Even her son gets frostbite when she's around."

"Have you tried Legal Aid?"

"I called them yesterday. They're swamped. It'll be a week before they can even talk to me."

"What did they tell you to do?"

"Go to a women's shelter."

An idea was forming in my head. I carried our cups to the counter for refills, giving the thought time to take shape. And giving myself time to decide whether I really wanted to act on it.

Cassie looked up from her sand castle, waved at her mother. I had a sudden flash of *déjà vu*. Laurie, a flower in a nursery-school pageant, flapping a leafy hand at me.

I decided I wanted to do it.

"I'm going to make a suggestion." I set Roxanne's cup in front of her and sat down with my own. "Hear me out. When I'm finished, you can say yes or no. Okay?"

"Sure."

"First. We go to the motel. You check out. Is there enough gas in your car to get to a gas station?"

"Maybe. Barely."

"You fill up and follow me home. Then I take you and Cassie to a shopping mall. You call the police. You tell them you were driven around for a couple of hours by the bank robber, then dumped at the mall. You tell them you're separated from your husband, that you live with your Aunt Catherine. Me. You tell them I dropped you off at the bank this morning. That I planned to pick you up later. They'll question you. They'll bring you home. To my place. You'll stay until Legal Aid can get you out of the mess you're in. We'll have to round out the details as we go along, but that's the gist of it."

I picked up my coffee cup and sipped, looking over the rim into her eyes. "Your turn. Yes or no."

Several expressions had flitted across her face. The last one, suspicion, remained. We eyed one another.

"Why?" she asked bluntly.

"Why?" I set my cup down. "I've been where you are. And I owe you for what I put you through this morning. I have . . . I had a child."

She sat unmoving, eyes narrowed, then said dryly, "Some kind of bank robber you are."

"Yes or no?"

"Yes. And thank you. I think."

I emptied my wallet. Her cheeks flushed when I handed her the money.

"Don't be silly," I said. "Put your mind to how we're going to keep Cassie from spilling the beans."

"Don't worry about Cassie," she assured me. "One thing. I'd really like to know. What made you rob a bank? Forgive me, but it seems such a . . . an insane thing to do. And you don't strike me as being that much of a nut."

"I'll tell you my sad story on the way," I promised.

11

Without counting the money, I slid the canvas bag far under my bed, together with the dress, the wig and the shoes. I had no idea of how much time I had before the police would arrive with Roxanne and Cassie.

The few clothes in Roxanne's one suitcase looked skimpy in Laurie's closet. I added a few of my own. Cassie's lone stuffed bear didn't do much to make the house look child-inhabited. I searched through the basement and found a box containing coloring books and crayons from Laurie's childhood and scattered them on the living-room floor. I dug up a squeaky plastic pig Brandy had disdained and placed it on the front step. It wasn't enough, but it would have to do.

I washed my face clean of makeup, pinned my hair back in a tight roll and ferreted through the linen closet until I found an apron. The police car turned into the driveway as I was tying it around my waist. I ran to the front door and threw it open.

Two officers stepped out of the car, Roxanne emerged from the rear seat carrying Cassie. I launched into a senior-citizen tizzy.

"Roxanne!" I screeched. "Where have you been? I've been going out of my mind! What happened? I went back twice looking for you. Where did you go? I've been going crazy with worry!"

I turned on the officer nearest. "Has there been an accident? Why are you here? Roxanne, why have the police brought you home? Is it Wayne? Has Wayne been causing trouble? Officer, I demand to know what's going on here!"

"Ma'am," the younger police officer tried to interrupt my flow. "If you'll—"

"Is Cassie all right?" I overrode him shrilly. "For heaven's sake, Roxanne, what's going on? Why are the police here? I've been out of my mind! I was about to call the police myself!"

Brandy stared at me as if she'd never seen me before and started howling. Cassie burst into a piercing wail. I snatched her from Roxanne's arms. "Officer, I demand to know what's going on! Do you hear me?"

The young officer had drawn Roxanne aside. He talked quietly to her, keeping a wary eye in my direction. She nodded and he hurried away to the patrol car, his partner at his heels.

"Officers!" I was beginning to enjoy my role. "Don't you dare leave! Do you hear me? I'm a tax payer! I pay your salaries and I demand to know what you've done to my niece!"

By then, I was playing to a diminished audience. The police car escaped with a squeal of tires. When it peeled off into the street, I handed Cassie back to Roxanne.

She eyed me with more than a trace of apprehension in her expression. "What was all that!"

"That was a takeoff on my Aunt Nell." I thought about it. "As a matter of fact, that was one hell of a good takeoff on my Aunt Nell."

Roxanne shook her head. "Awesome," she said.

12

"Exactly thirty-seven thousand, two hundred and fourteen dollars." I squared off a block of hundred-dollar bills.

"Is it enough?" Roxanne glanced over her shoulder at the money on the kitchen table. She wedged the last plate into the dishwasher and latched the door.

"More than enough." I counted off $2,214 in bills and set them aside. The remaining $35,000 I replaced in the canvas bag. "This goes in my safety deposit box tomorrow. I'll be damned if I'll turn it over to Mort until one minute before the deadline."

I went to the bedroom, replaced the bag under my bed. I returned to the kitchen with a brown kraft envelope and a felt-tipped pen, dug a paper grocery bag and a pair of rubber gloves out of a kitchen drawer. Roxanne watched with quizzical eyes as I cut a letter-sized square from the paper bag. Her puzzlement grew when I pulled on the rubber gloves and wiped the page clean with a damp cloth. Using my left hand and the felt-tipped pen I wrote a clumsy note.

" 'I only needed thirty-five thousand dollars. Thank you," she read aloud. "I don't get it," she said. "What're you doing?"

"I'm giving the rest back." I began wiping the bills clean, both sides. "I am not a crook, to quote what'sisname."

"I don't believe it." Roxanne stared. "I just don't believe this. Why?"

"Because if I keep one penny more than Mort is stealing from me, they'll get me." I stuffed $2,214 into the kraft envelope and sealed it. I wrote BANK MANAGER in large block letters across the face, then wiped the envelope clean. I stood up.

"I'm going to drop this off in the night deposit. How about coffee when I get back?"

"Actually," Roxanne summed up her experience with the police, "they were pretty decent. They promised not to release my name unless it becomes necessary. They asked me, politely, to keep myself available if I was needed to identify you."

I stared at her across the kitchen table, horrified by the sudden realization of the position I had drawn her into.

"How could I have been so stupid?" I groaned. "I should have had the police drop you at the motel. Do you realize if they get me, you're dead too? Damn. Damn. How could I have been so stupid?"

"Hey! Relax. They're not going to get you. The black woman is convinced it was a man dressed up as a woman. A couple of the tellers think so too. And I didn't discourage the idea."

"I should never have got you into this. You weren't—"

"Catherine!" she interrupted sharply. "You didn't get me into anything! I made the decision to tag along. It's the first positive decision I've made in three years. I've been trying to get up the guts to leave Wayne since Cassie was born. You may have provided the impetus, but the decision was mine."

"And if it turns out to have been a lousy decision?"

"Then I'm stuck with it. Just like you are."

"I had nothing to lose I wasn't going to lose anyway. That's my excuse. What's yours?"

For a moment she was startled, then she laughed. "You

know why I went along? Because you offered us a place to stay until I could force Wayne to let me get my things out of the house.''

''I've been thinking about that. Is there any way we can get into the house?''

''I don't think so. Wayne has the keys and he's not answering my calls.''

''Forget Wayne. If we can get into—''

''Wait!'' Her eyes gleamed. ''The shed!''

''Shed?''

''There's a garden-equipment shed at the back of the house, with a door to the basement.'' She leaned forward, excitement in her voice. ''He didn't change the lock on the shed door because there's a slide bolt on the door to the basement. Inside. And I still have the key to the shed.''

''So if we can slide that bolt, we can get in?''

She slumped. ''Yeah. But we have to get in to slide the bolt. And if we could get into the place to slide the bolt, we wouldn't have to slide the goddamn bolt.''

''Roxanne. The house is for sale.''

''So?'' She frowned at me.

''So I'm Mrs. Oscar Wilde. I'm looking to buy a house. I call the agent. Who's the agent?''

''Guess.''

''Dorothy what'sername?''

She pointed a finger at me.

''So in the morning, I phone what'sername. She shows the house. I slide the bolt. We go back and clean the place out.''

Roxanne tilted back in her chair. She crossed her arms over her breasts and looked at me askance.

''You know what we're talking about?'' She was smiling a cat's sly smile. ''Breaking and entering. Burglary. They can send us to jail for burglary.''

I smiled back. ''They'll have to get in line.''

13

I strolled into the kitchen dressed in a garage-sale Liz Claiborne raw silk suit, rummage-sale Gucci snakeskin handbag and the buttery-soft leather Amalfi pumps from my halcyon days. I had applied makeup sparingly: blush, a touch of coral lipstick, blue eyeliner. A spritz of *L'Air du Temps* cologne.

Roxanne glanced up from the morning paper. Her brows lifted. "Hot-diggidy-dog," she said.

"Hot-diggidy-dog? You're way too young to know hot-diggidy-dog."

"My grandfather's highest accolade. You look absolutely smashing. And impressive. And expensive."

"What I look like is an aging yuppie. Think Atkins will buy it?"

"She'll drool." Roxanne tapped the newspaper. "You got two paragraphs on page nine. The police, it says here, are searching for a middle-aged man, five-foot-ten, approximately a hundred and sixty pounds. Five-ten? One-sixty? All I could see was that godawful dress." She grinned suddenly. "Which is probably why you wore it?"

"*Trompe l'oeil.* Deception of the eye? Distraction, actually. Where's Cassie?"

"Out on the patio. She's giving Brandy a perm."

Brandy lay sprawled in the shade of the oak tree, her ruff abloom with pink and blue plastic curlers Cassie was rolling into her fur. I watched for a moment and felt a stab of loss. Laurie. Oh, my sweet Laurie, where did it all go?

"There's a swing in the basement." I turned back to

Roxanne. "It's probably hanging on one of the hooks above the oil tank. If you like, we can hang it from one of the lower branches of the oak tree." I glanced at my watch. "I have to leave now, but if you can find it, we can put it up when I get back."

"I'll look for it." Roxanne rose from the table and walked with me to the car. She held up both hands, fingers crossed, as I turned the ignition.

"Break a leg," she called.

I drove out the driveway, automatically glancing into the rearview mirror. Behind me, a black car pulled away from the curb. My heart beat three loud thumps. I considered flooring the gas pedal and running like hell. Then sanity took over.

There is only one person in this black car. There have to be a billion black cars, probably a million in this city alone. I'm becoming paranoid about black cars.

I turned left on a green light. The black car sped through the orange and fell in behind me. Fourteen blocks and five turns later, it was still there and I was beginning to lose my grip on common sense.

At Half-Moon Crescent, Roxanne's street, I turned right and parked. The black car continued on along Elmwood Avenue and I let out a *whoosh* of pent-up breath. Coincidence.

I was early. I sat in the car and studied the crescent.

It was well named, a half moon with five houses on the rim of the crescent, each facing onto a central parklike area—simply a grassy sward, with no trees or shrubs to screen the view from one house to another. Roxanne's house was second from the left, a flipflop design of the houses on either side, typical of suburban houses built by a single contractor.

As I got out of the car and crossed the park, a maroon sedan turned into the crescent, rounded the half circle and parked in front of Roxanne's house.

A tall, slim blond woman in a dove-gray suit stepped out. She reached in for her briefcase, then turned and caught sight of me. One swift, appraising glance from my hair to my shoes. Then a wide, practised smile that didn't reach her slightly protuberant, stone-washed, denim-blue eyes. Her long, pale hair was carefully arranged in unbrushed strings, that slovenly style which reminds me of the mythical Medusa whose locks were changed into serpents by the vengeful goddess Minerva. Yuk.

"You must be Mrs. Wilde." She extended her hand. "I'm Mrs. Atkins. Am I late?"

"No, no. I'm early. I'm one of those compulsively punctual people. Which means I'm always early, of course." *Chatty Cathy.* "I drove my husband mad for years! But then, of course, William was one of those people who'd be late for his own funeral."

She laughed merrily as though I'd said something witty. Or original.

"Why don't we go inside?" She dug into her large ostrich handbag, searching for keys. "You mentioned you're looking for a home for your daughter?"

"They're being transferred. For the third time. Actually, I'm eliminating houses I know won't suit Laurie." I pasted on a smug little smile. "Laurie trusts my taste completely, you know. It's amazing how much alike our tastes are. But then, of course, the apple doesn't fall far from the tree, does it?"

"Here we are." She inserted the key in the lock. "I'm sure you'll like this home, Mrs. Wilde." She smiled brilliantly. "It's one of the most attractive homes on our list."

It's a house, lady. You buy a house. You make a home.

Inside, the air was heavy and stale. The living room was empty of furnishings. On the floor, five sad plants drooped, leaves yellowing.

"The wall-to-wall carpeting goes with the house," she announced and began her tour, spieling as she led me from one room to another. She explained the presence of the clothing in the closets, price tags on the few remaining pieces of furniture.

"They haven't entirely moved out. They've had a moving sale. The rest of the stuff—" she gestured at the drapes, the pictures "—will go into a garage sale this coming weekend."

Following her through the kitchen—no fridge, no stove—to the basement stairwell, I knew that while I would finish going through the motions, the entire exercise was turning out to be a waste of time. Except for the clothing, which could be replaced, there was nothing in the house worth coming back for.

The door to the shed was where Roxanne had said it would be, in the laundry room, next to the dryer. The bolt was a foot above the floor.

Atkins eulogized the concrete sink, the tile floor and the superior plumbing. I barely heard her. Shoot the bolt or forget it? I looked out the window above the dryer. Yes or no? There was a vase on the sill filled with dried flowers. I glanced at it, then actually looked at it and felt a tingle of excitement.

"What a funny vase." I flipped my fingers at the window.

"Isn't it hideous?" Atkins wrinkled her nose and gestured at the storage room behind her. "There's a lot of old junk like that in there. Garage-sale junk. The room will be cleared, of course." She opened the storage door. "Built-in shelving. And a good-sized storage area."

"Oh, yes. It is, isn't it? So important, plenty of space for storing things. Most builders overlook adequate facility for all those things you have to put somewhere."

I babbled on about the importance of storage space, my eye on a beer stein perched on one of the shelves, my mind skittering for a way to shoot that damn bolt. Drop my purse? Trip on a crack in the tile? Swoon?

"Dorothy?" The call came from upstairs, a male voice.

Atkins glanced at her watch, dazzled a smile at me. "Would you excuse me for just a moment? I'll be right back."

"Please!" I waved an airy dismissal. "Take your time! I'll just look around by my own little self."

"I won't be a moment. I promise." Another sparkling display of teeth and she was gone, tripping lightly up the stairs.

I leaped at the bolt and slid it back, pushed a white wicker laundry basket in front of the door, dashed to the storage room, picked up the stein, saw the mark, smiled to myself and strolled to the stairs.

Halfway up, I caught her words.

". . . suitcases are in my car." The dulcet tones were gone. She was snarling. "What the hell's the matter with you, Wayne? I distinctly remember telling you to meet me at home. Why the hell can't you do as you're told?"

I brought my foot down heavily on the next step and trilled her name.

"Mrs. Atkins? I've decided. I love the house." I reached the top of the stairs, simpering, "And I think Laurie will adore it."

She turned quickly. "I'm sure she will, Mrs. Wilde."

"She'll be here tomorrow. I'd like her to see it as soon as possible. Tomorrow?"

"I'm sorry, Mrs. Wilde." The dazzling smile. "But, as I mentioned on the phone, I'll be out of town this weekend."

"Oh?" I injected a little frost into the word. "Then perhaps the owner?"

"This gentleman is the owner," she gestured. "Mrs. Wilde. Mr. Parker."

Wayne Parker was tall and almost handsome. He was a man who required animation to appear attractive, who would not photograph well. His blond hair was thinning above a narrow face. His eyes were a pale watercolor blue,

set a shade too close to a nose that just missed being pug-
gish. His wide smile revealed a Kennedy mouthful of
square white teeth. His handshake was too firm and he held
my hand a moment too long.

And he was wearing too much *Brut* cologne.

"How do you do, Mrs. Wilde." His voice had the carefully practised depth of a third-rate television announcer.
"I'm so pleased that you like my home."

"Oh, I do, Mr. Parker," I assured him. "But then, of
course, the decision wouldn't be mine. The house is for my
daughter. She has to see it first. Tomorrow, if possible."

"Unfortunately, I won't be available over the weekend."
He produced a rueful smile. "A business conference out of
town. But I'm sure Mrs. Atkins would be happy to meet
with your daughter on Monday?"

"Certainly." She darted a look at him that should have
left a welt on his face. He picked up his exit cue and left.

"I'd like to see the back garden," I said to Atkins when
the door closed on him. "Laurie and Andy are into gardening and she's sure to ask about the back yard."

"Of course."

She checked the lock on the back shed, as I'd been sure
she would. She didn't unlock the shed and check the basement door as I'd been fearful she might. I cooed over the
back yard and we returned to the front of the house.

"I'll call you first thing Monday morning," I promised as
we parted, she to her car, I to mine. I waited until she
turned into Elmwood before I drove away.

14

*R*oxanne was on the patio steelwooling fire-extinguisher scum from a drum table. I pushed the screen door open.

"You don't have to do that," I said.

She looked up, smiled. "Hi!" She dropped the steelwool pad and moved the table into the shade. "Sit yourself down. There's fresh coffee. I'll just be a minute."

I sank into a chair and toed my shoes off. The swing hung from the old oak tree. Roxanne had put it up without my help. Cassie and Brandy were down by the cedar hedge playing with a ball. Overhead, a family of sparrows argued raucously. The scent of lilacs was heavy in the sun-warmed air.

I'm not going to lose my house.

"A very sweet man named Charles called." Roxanne pushed her way through the screen door with a tray in her hands. "He must have apologized at least ten times. Anyway, he said he had a live one for the Sheraton crossbanded table and could he please please please have it Monday. I told him if he could describe it, chances are he could have it. Can he?" I nodded and she continued. "It's one hell of a mess down there. I'll clean off the crud. He said you have two other pieces for him."

"A tripod table and a basin stand. I know. But you don't have to clean the crud," I said.

"I don't have to do anything but breathe or die. But I'll still clean off the crud." She handed me my coffee cup, leaned back in her chair and said, "So?"

"Mission accomplished. But unless what I think is there is really there, it isn't worth going back in."

I described, as nearly as I could remember, the contents of the house, room by room. She listened, not interrupting. When I finished, she said very quietly, "The bastard."

"Most of the stuff I don't give a damn about," she went on after a moment. "But Grandma's Royal Doultons and her oak china cabinet, those I liked."

"No Doultons. No china cabinet. But." I set my coffee cup down. "There's a vase filled with dried flowers on the windowsill in the laundry room. Are there any more like it in the storage room?"

"The Clarice Cliff? Yes. There are quite a few pieces. She was a friend of my grandmother's. Why?"

I gaped at her. "Clarice Cliff was a friend of your grandmother's? My God, that's like saying Tiffany's an old buddy." She frowned and I waved it aside. "Never mind. The stein I saw in the storage room. Any more of those?"

She nodded. "Eight of them, I think. At least. They were my grandfather's. He collected steins."

"Eight! Who *were* your grandparents?" She looked puzzled. "I mean, where'd they get this stuff?"

"Faultbooting around Europe."

"Faultbooting?"

"That's what my grandfather told me. He said it means touring. Anyway, it seems he and my grandmother did a lot of faultbooting in their time. I always thought it sounded lewd."

I couldn't help laughing. "Good for them. Better for you. That stein happens to be a Mettlach. And old Mettlachs can go as high as three thousand dollars. Each. And that Clarice Cliff is probably worth anywhere from five to eight hundred dollars. Or maybe more."

It was her turn to stare. "Are you serious?"

"We've got to get it all out this weekend. Tomorrow. They're having a garage sale next weekend."

"A garage sale? They're selling my things in a garage sale?"

"They've already sold most of your things in a moving sale." I leaned on my elbows and looked squarely at her. "Let's cut to the chase. Do we or don't we?"

"I will if you will. I don't think I have the guts to do it alone."

"You don't have to do it alone." I stood up. "Okay. We do it. I've got a phone call to make."

The answering machine clicked in on the third ring. I was giving my name at the beep when Steve's voice cut in.

"Hey, Cat. I'm here."

"Hi, Steve. How's the book going?"

"Like shitting a brick," he said glumly. "Need something delivered?"

"Not delivered. Moved. Tomorrow morning. Can you do it?"

"How much. How far."

"Not too much. Not enough to fill your van. You pick it up about fifteen blocks away and bring it here."

"Just a sec." I heard him mutter *Saturday, Saturday.* "Okay. I've only got one place tomorrow. You said morning. What time?"

"Seven ayem?"

"Get outta here, Cat."

"When?"

"I guess I can do the other place first. How does ten o'clock sound?"

"Ten's fine." I gave him the address and returned to the patio.

"Steve will be there at ten," I told Roxanne. "If we leave early, we can have it all packed and ready by then."

"Who's Steve?"

"Steve Troyan. He's an old friend. He's a landscaper, but he delivers the pieces I work on that won't fit in my car."

"An old friend." Roxanne frowned dubiously. "Did you tell him what we're doing?"

"Don't worry about Steve. Worry about the neighbors. Are any of them likely to tell Wayne if they see you emptying out the place?"

Roxanne's eyes widened. "The neighbors. Oh boy. Let me think. The Andersons, he's a professor. They're in Europe. Sabbatical. The Changs are never home. They own a fruit store. The Sawyers go to their cottage every weekend. Frieda Hoffman. She's the only one who could be a problem. She's the neighborhood snoop. She also has the hots for Wayne, little does she know. Can we be out of there before noon?"

"I think so. Why?"

"She's a night nurse at Lakeshore General. She gets home around noon."

"We should be long gone by then."

15

*D*riving through the early Saturday-morning streets, I asked Roxanne what Wayne's reaction to our raid would be.

"Not pleasant." She spoke quietly. Cassie was in the rear seat with Brandy. "Wayne loves buzz phrases like 'I don't get mad, I get even.' He'll probably get both. Mad and mean." Her face darkened. "I'm not stealing anything. All I'm taking is what belongs to me."

"Even so. We're breaking into a locked house. Wayne will probably know it's you by what's missing. If he wants to be vindictive . . ." I didn't finish the thought. "I have an idea. If you want to hear it."

"Of course I want to hear it."

"We trash the house."

"We what?"

"That policeman, what was his name? Quinn? When those kids wrecked my house, he said they were expressing their displeasure at not getting cash and booze. Suppose kids broke into your house and didn't find any money or liquor? They'd probably do the same. Quinn said there wasn't much chance of the police ever finding out who did it."

Roxanne nodded thoughtfully. "Go on."

"So far as I could see, the only things of value were in the storage room. Your grandparents' stuff. We take it all. Anything else, you choose only what you really want. Pick the clothes you like, scatter the rest all over the place. Tell Cassie she can take a couple of toys. We wreck the kitchen the way those kids did mine. We trash the place." I glanced at her. "What do you think?"

"I think it's a lousy thing to do. Let's do it."

We set Cassie up with a small box and instructions to fill it. Brandy watched her fill the box, change her mind and empty it, then stretched out and fell asleep.

Roxanne selected two skirts, a sweater and a leather jacket from a meager wardrobe and strewed the rest around the room with abandon. The night tables, the lamps and framed prints were tossed in a pile. I tied a knot in the curtains.

"I'll do the bathrooms," I told her. "Go in the den, pack up the books you want and heave the others around."

I finished the bathrooms, went to the kitchen. I opened all the cupboard doors, pulled out every drawer and began by pouring corn syrup into a drawer full of kitchen utensils. I dropped the empty bottle on the floor and looked up to see Roxanne standing in the doorway, an expression of shock on her face. I handed her a canister of sugar. She looked down at it helplessly.

"Think of it this way," I said. I took the canister from her and upended it, dumping the gritty contents on the floor. "You won't have to clean it up. Wayne and cluck-face will have to. Or hire someone to do it."

We wrecked the kitchen together, kicked over the wilted plants in the living room, then went down to the basement. We dragged bits and pieces of furniture and empty cartons into the storage room to replace the boxes we removed, then pushed the steel shelves down. They fell with a satisfying crash.

By ten o'clock, everything we were taking was piled in the upstairs hall. Eleven cartons. Cassie's bed, Roxanne's desk. There was nothing else worthwhile.

I handed the thermos to Roxanne. "Pour us some coffee. I'll be back in a minute. There's something I forgot to do."

I went out to the back yard and kicked in the window to the laundry room. Then I went down to the basement and shot the bolt back in place.

When I returned, Roxanne was eyeing the assorted boxes and crates moodily, her hands clasped around a mug of coffee.

"Six years of marriage." She gestured with her chin. "Not much to show for it, is there?"

"Well. What the hell." I poured coffee, creaked wearily down to the floor and leaned against the wall. "Better six years than sixteen."

"I guess."

Roxanne squatted on her heels beside me. We were silent, contemplating the detritus of her marriage. She tilted her head, looking down at me.

"You didn't tell me what you thought of Wayne."

"Not much. He's a Bob."

"What's a bob?"

"Bob. My husband. Scratch the surface and what you've got underneath is a shitty character." I finished my coffee. "In Bob's case, no character. Just a massive thirst."

"Thirst? He was an alcoholic?"

"He was a drunk."

"What's the difference?"

"No difference. I just think alcoholic is a cop-out word for a drunk."

"Isn't alcoholism supposed to be a disease?"

"Sure it is. Tell that to anybody who's been messed up by a real live drunkard."

"You don't think it's a disease?"

"I think it's a symptom. I think all excesses and obsessions are symptoms of a character problem. Something missing. Something flawed."

"So what was the problem?"

"Bob's?" I leaned my head against the wall, remembering the gutted feeling of failure. Remembering, even long after

65

I ran, the sleepless nights of self-flagellation. What had I done I shouldn't have done? Or could have done that I didn't do? What had I said I shouldn't . . . *mea culpa, mea culpa.* . . .

"When we met, Bob was young and good-looking and funny and fun. Everything came easy. Then life got real. It wasn't all fun and games anymore. So he hid out in bars trading lies with all the other boozers, pretending he was actually doing something constructive."

"What was the flaw?"

"It took me a long time to pin down the right word for Bob's flaw. Then I found *sloth* and it was right on. Sloth is a disinclination to labor. That was Bob. Very disinclined to labor."

"Sloth." Roxanne tilted her head. "Now there's a word with a nice old-timey ring to it. How about *lucre?*"

"Lucre? As in money?"

"Money. You say obsessions are symptoms. That's Wayne's obsession. Money."

"Money to have? Or money to spend?"

"Spend? Wayne?" Roxanne snorted. "Believe me, Catherine, Wayne would rather open a vein than his wallet."

I laughed. Roxanne cast a startled glance at me, then grinned. She let her long legs slide down and sat sprawled against the wall beside me, looking like a lanky doll cast aside by a careless child.

"I might be exaggerating," she conceded. "But not by a hell of a lot. That's what he married me for. Money."

"You had money?"

She rolled her head against the wall in a gesture of denial. "My grandparents. My grandfather was a stockbroker. My grandmother was a buyer for a chain of boutiques. Big bucks. Plus expense accounts. Plus every credit card you ever heard of. Sort of 'Lifestyles of the Rich and Famous' on a minor scale." Roxanne smiled a dry smile. "Poor Wayne. He thought it was for real. So he married me."

I thought of Wayne's close-set eyes and pompous diction. "Why did you marry him?"

"Probably because I was the only twenty-year-old virgin I knew. And horny."

"You were a twenty-year-old virgin? I thought the sexual revolution made virginity illegal in anyone over sixteen."

"Twelve." Roxanne side-glanced at me scornfully. "Where have you been living? The legal age limit is twelve now."

"Twelve? Sweet Jesus." I shook my head. "I have a feeling I've lived too long. So? What happened?"

"Happened?"

"To the money. To the marriage. To you."

Roxanne brought her knees up and leaned her crossed arms on them. She dropped her chin on her forearms and gazed pensively at her sneakered feet.

"They died in North Carolina. My grandparents. A head-on collision with a couple of spaced-out kids joyriding a stolen car. Stupid, stupid. So damn senseless. Friday morning, they played golf. Friday night, they were dead."

Roxanne was silent. I glanced at my watch. Eleven-ten. Where was Steve?

"They didn't have a dime." Roxanne frowned as though it was still impossible for her to believe it. "The way they lived? So help me, they didn't have a dime. The house was sold to pay off bank loans. All the credit cards. I kept a few pieces of furniture, those boxes, my grandmother's car. Everything else went to pay for their funerals."

"You said he was a stockbroker. Your grandfather. No stocks? No bonds? No gilt-edged investment portfolios?"

"No nothing. Not even insurance policies. Wayne went ape. The way he carried on, you'd swear they'd cheated him, blown money that belonged to him. He'd always been a slow man with a buck. I knew that. But when he realized there wasn't going to be any payoff, he gave stingy a whole new meaning. That's when Cassie was born." She turned her head to face me. She started to speak, changed her mind.

"What?" I asked.

She grimaced, then asked hesitantly, "Did your husband ever hit you?"

"Hit me? Bob?" The question caught me by surprise. I smiled at her. "Once. I told him if it ever happened again, I'd wait till he was dead drunk and cut his balls off."

She blinked, then giggled. "Would you have done it? I mean, would you have *really* done it?"

"I'll never know. He believed me. Why? Has Wayne ever hit you?"

"I can't say he's ever really hit me . . . I'm not a battered wife or anything like that." Her brows drew together and she tilted her head. "But he was always hurting me. D'you know what I mean?"

"No. How was he always hurting you?"

"Well . . . like . . . he'd drop a hammer on my bare foot, for instance. Or open a cupboard door so I'd bang my head. Or flush the toilet when I was showering and I'd get scalding water. I once had a black eye when he turned over in his sleep and got me with his fist. Once he closed the car door on my fingers. It was always accidental. Do you know what I mean? Somehow it was always an accident."

"Accident? For God's sake, Roxanne, the man's not only a cheapskate, he's a wife abuser! Why in the world did you stay with him?"

Roxanne was silent, frowning unseeing at her toes. Then she shrugged. "Yeah. Why. Maybe because my mother was a flower child? Whatever a flower child was." She tilted her head at me. "You were around then. What the hell was a flower child?"

"Flower child?" I sent my mind back to the sixties, that turbulent decade. "Silly young girls in tatty caftans. Granny glasses. Bare feet and naked faces. Ironed hair.

Communes, everybody screwing anybody who asked. Make love, not war."

"Uh-huh. I guess that was my mama. A silly young girl who got herself knocked up at seventeen, had me at eighteen and bled to death from a botched abortion when she was nineteen."

"Oh." I was startled by her matter-of-fact tone. "I'm sorry."

"Don't be." Roxanne shook her head. "I never knew her. Or much about her. I'd ask my grandmother what she was like, but the most I got was that she was a great disappointment to them. I guess I stopped asking. I asked about my father just once. They told me the one and only thing they knew about him. He was white."

I laughed. I couldn't help it. Roxanne glanced at me with amused eyes.

"My grandparents weren't big on sentiment," she said in a dry voice.

I was surprised by a sudden flare of anger. "I don't mean to knock your grandparents," I said, "but they don't strike me as having been all that big on tenderness and understanding, either."

The humor fled from Roxanne's eyes.

"I'm not blaming my grandparents. They'd already done the daughter thing. They had their own lives. I learned to walk and talk in a day-care center. Then I was packed off to boarding school. And that's the story of my childhood. Boarding schools and summer camps. Expensive boarding schools and summer camps. I wasn't exactly underprivileged." Her lips thinned. "But I know all about growing up—"

The doorbell shrilled. Roxanne flinched.

"Hey. Relax," I reassured her. "It's Steve."

Brandy came loping down the hall, followed by Cassie. I went to the door and opened it. Steve grinned down at me.

"I know, Cat." He held up both hands, palms out. "I'm late. I had to take—"

"Forget it. You're here now. Steve, this is Roxanne. And Cassie. Let's get this show on the road."

"It's nice to see you too, Cat." He kissed my cheek. "Hello, Roxanne. Hi, Cassie. Hey, Brandy, how's my girl?"

Steve is a six-footer, lean in the hips, broad in the shoulders. Without being handsome, he's immensely attractive, due mainly to a grab-bag collection of features thrown together in a way that works. He has chestnut hair, sun-streaked now, razor-cut to fall in deep waves to the nape of his neck. He inherited high cheekbones from his Cossack great-grandfather, a classic Roman nose from an Italian grandmother and a firm, stubborn chin from his Irish mother. A deep tan fails to hide the dimple in one corner of his perfect white smile. His eyes are that foggy shade of gray that seems to pick up color from its surroundings. Today they were pale turquoise, reflecting the faded T-shirt he was wearing. They're eyes you can see into, warm and humorous.

He's intelligent. He has a sense of humor. He's funny. And he's a person before he's a male, which means he never feels he has to prove anything, to women or to himself.

And I wish, every time I see him, that I'd met him forty years ago.

"We'll chat later," I said brusquely. "Is the van open? We have to be out of here by noon." I picked up a box. "Let's do it, shall we?"

"Keep your shirt on, Cat." Steve winked at Cassie and took the box from me. "I'll unlock the van. Get everything together and we can start."

"Everything's here."

He scanned the hallway. "This is it? Hell, we'll be out of here in ten minutes."

He went out to the van. Cassie watched him go and turned to me, her face clouded.

"Are you really a cat?" she asked.

"Cat? Oh. No, I'm not a cat. Steve calls me Cat because he punched me into his computer as WILDE.CAT. That's just Steve's idea of funny."

Cassie's eyes widened. "Did he punch you?"

"No. No, honey. It's just a way of saying he put me into his computer."

"What's a computer?"

"It's a . . . a what? It's a machine."

"Did he put you in a machine?"

I looked at Roxanne. She was grinning.

"I'd forgotten this part," I said. "No, honey," I assured Cassie. "Steve didn't put me in a machine. How about I explain it all to you when we get home, okay? Right now we have work to do. I think your job will be to keep Brandy out of our way. D'you think you can do that?"

I picked up a box and carried it out to the van.

Steve came in, Roxanne carried a box out. Steve carried a box out. I returned, stepping aside to let Steve pass. Roxanne waited. Cassie and Brandy trailed everybody in and out, creating a bottleneck in the doorway.

"Hold it." Steve ducked around Brandy. "Let's get a system going here. First, we get the desk out. Then, Cat, you get into the van. I'll carry the stuff out of the house and give it to Roxanne at the bottom of the stairs. Roxanne gives it to Cat. Cat places it into the van. And you, Short Stuff," he squatted down to Cassie's level, "you take this here doggone dog over to that there little park and show her how grass grows."

Cassie frowned into his face. "My name is Cassie."

"You damn right it is." Steve tapped her nose. "And don't you forget it."

The system worked fine. We were three boxes short of the load when Steve failed to appear. We waited.

"What the hell?" Roxanne muttered finally. I stepped

down from the van and we went back into the house to investigate the delay.

Steve stood in the empty living room, staring intently out the big picture window. He turned as we entered.

"Okay, Cat." He was as close to anger as I'd ever seen him. "Suppose you tell me what the hell's going on here."

"What do you mean?"

"I mean all that shit in there." He thumbed toward the kitchen. "Yeah, I looked around. I mean the big hurry to get out. I mean the clown out there taking pictures."

"Pictures?" I gaped. "What clown?"

"He was parked when I came. He's been sitting in his car taking pictures ever since."

"Where?" I rushed to the window, my heart thudding.

"He just left. I thought he might be some real-estate character. Except he wasn't taking pictures of the house. He was taking shots of us. So what I want to know right now is, what's going down here?"

"Was it a black car?"

"What the hell difference does it make what color the car was?" Steve glared at me. "Yes. It was a black car. A black Jag. Forget the goddamn car. I want to know just what the hell I'm involved in here."

I glanced down at my watch. Almost twelve. *Black car?*

"Steve?" I bit my lip. "Look, Steve. Do you trust me?"

"Now and then. Mostly then."

"Believe me, Steve. There's a logical explanation. I'll fill you in when we get to my place. I'll cook you a truly gorgeous lunch and explain. Right now, pardon me, but we've got to *get the fuck out of here.*"

He blinked, then grinned. "What kind of gorgeous lunch?"

I gave him the classic palm-up gesture. He chortled, picked up two boxes and ambled out the door. Roxanne snatched up the last box. I set the door to lock and closed it behind me.

Steve latched the rear door of the van, waved to us and drove away. Roxanne bundled Cassie and Brandy into the back seat of my car, then jumped into the passenger seat. I started the motor and we were rolling down toward Elmwood when a blue Honda turned into the crescent. Roxanne slid down in her seat, whacking her knees on the dashboard.

"*Shit*," she moaned. "That hurt. The blue car is Frieda. Do you think she saw me?"

"I don't think so." The only car I was worried about was black. *Taking pictures?*

"What are you going to tell him?"

"Who? Steve? The truth. Is that a problem?"

"No. Yes. He'll think I . . ." Her shoulders lifted. "Hell, I don't know. It's just that it all sounds so . . . so tacky. I've always hated people whose lives read like some damn soap opera."

"Roxanne, believe me. Everybody's life reads like some damn soap opera. Including Steve's. Don't worry about Steve. He's been there and back."

"How do you mean?"

"Steve was creative director with an advertising agency I did a lot of freelance work for." I smiled at Roxanne. "A big wheel. He was married. To a gorgeous creature named Lisa, who was public relations director for a cosmetics firm. Lisa wasn't only a knockout, she was a very bright cookie. And nice, nice, nice. Everybody liked Lisa. Steve was crazy about her."

"Did you like her?"

"Then?" I held my hand level, palm down, and tilted it from side to side. "So-so. Anyway. Two of Steve's friends at the agency died in the same year. His art director from bleeding ulcers. One of the VP's of a heart attack. Both men were in their forties. It shook Steve. He'd started out as a copywriter. He was always going to write seriously. Someday. Those two dying, I think it hit him there are no guarantees on someday, and he began making sounds about getting out. Doing something that would leave him with more time and mental energy to write. I must admit I didn't believe he'd ever do it."

"Why not?"

"Money maybe. Lisa maybe."

"Was she against it?"

"If she was, she was too smart to say so. Then Steve's father died and left him a house out in the boonies. And a pickup truck and gardening equipment. So he did it. He quit. And after his last day with the agency, he went home to an empty apartment. I mean literally empty. No Lisa, no nothing. She'd cleaned out the safety deposit box, their bank account and the apartment. Walked out with everything but his shorts. Didn't even leave a note."

"Bitch. What did Steve do?"

"He holed up in his father's house. Dropped out for almost a year."

"Didn't he try to get any of it back?"

"He told me he'd had two options at the time. He could sue. Waste a lot of time and money. And the only winners would be the lawyers. Or he could apply his ass to a chair and write."

"Is he a good writer?"

"He's a very good writer. His first book sank without a trace and he didn't make a dime on it. But it was published."

"What was it about?"

"Murder." I grinned at Roxanne. "The victim is a blonde bimbo named Lisa. She's smeared with salmon mousse, tied up naked and dumped alive on a garbage scow crawling with rats."

Roxanne shuddered. "God. What would make him even think of anything so gruesome?"

"Lisa loved salmon mousse."

"Not now I bet."

"I think that was the general idea."

74

16

*S*teve was leaning against the van, his legs crossed, arms akimbo. He unfolded when I stepped out of the car.

"House or garage?" He thumbed at the van behind him.

"Garage." I lifted my eyebrows at Roxanne. "Except the boxes from the basement? We'll go through them and see what's there. Okay?"

An hour later, we sat down to Steve's favorite dish of potato pancakes with sour cream, a green salad and hot biscuits Roxanne had whipped together with impressive ease, and a bottle of chilled white wine.

While we ate, Steve described a computer to Cassie, with a promise to punch her into his as soon as she decided on a file name for herself. We invented silly names until Cassie wilted suddenly, her head drooping like a pink rose too heavy for its stem. Roxanne gathered her up and carried her off for a nap. Brandy, after gauging the probability of further handouts from the table, loped after them.

I was setting out coffee cups when Roxanne returned. She glanced uneasily at Steve, then sat down, clasped her hands around her cup and visibly braced herself.

"Okay, Cat." Steve tilted back in his chair, wedged his knee against the table and crossed his arms. "Let's have it."

I began with the anonymous letter Roxanne had received, the changed locks, the proposed garage sale. Roxanne sat immobile throughout, reacting only with a startled blink when I referred to Wayne as a twit and with a snicker when I described Dorothy Atkins as a bargain-basement Leona Helmsley.

Steve listened without comment. When I finished, he dropped his chair down.

"Okay." He turned on Roxanne. "I can see why you had to do it. What I don't understand is why you had to rope Cat into it."

Roxanne raised startled eyes to his face. "Me? Me rope in Catherine? Now that's funny."

"What's so funny about it?"

"Why don't you ask Catherine?"

Steve frowned, first at Roxanne, then at me. "Okay. Come on. What the hell's going on?"

"Okay." I took a deep breath. "The truth is, I met Roxanne while I was robbing a bank."

"Sure you did," Steve snorted. "Come on, Cat. Don't jerk me around. I'm serious."

"So am I. I robbed a bank." I pointed at Roxanne. "She and Cassie were my hostages. That's how we met."

"I don't believe you," Steve said flatly.

And suddenly, in a cosmic lurch of reality, I didn't believe it either. What did that demented old woman making faces at receptionists have to do with me? Plotting bank robberies and burglaries? Trashing houses and kicking in windows? Laurie would die if she knew.

That's not funny.

I shrugged. "It's true."

"When?" Steve eyed me askance, still not convinced. "Where? And for Christ's sake, why?"

I told him when and where. I told him everything about why. When I got to the how, he stared at me as if he'd never seen me before. I finished and waited.

"A plastic knife filled with ketchup?" He began to laugh, stopped abruptly. "What the hell am I laughing at? This is crazy! Bank robbery? Burglary? They're going to get you, Cat."

"They're not going to get me." The bank robbery

seemed long ago and far away. Five minutes in another life. "According to statistics, only one in five bank robbers are caught."

"They think it was a man in drag," Roxanne said. "It was the shoes. You had to see the shoes." She grinned at me. "Charlie Chaplin shoes."

"I'm thinking of having them bronzed."

"I don't believe this." Steve pushed away from the table. "Jokes yet. Don't either of you realize how serious this is? What you've done is illegal. You're criminals. People go to prison for what you've done. For Christ's sake, Cat."

"I couldn't lose my house. I'd rather go to prison than lose my house."

"It's not stealing to take your own things," Roxanne said. "And that's all we took. The stuff that belonged to me anyway."

I seized on the diversion.

"The boxes! Your grandparents' boxes. There's money in those boxes. I'm positive." I jumped to my feet. "I'll clean up. You and Steve go unpack the boxes. Go!"

Steve threw up his hands. He followed Roxanne from the kitchen, shaking his head.

I scraped the dishes and stashed them in the dishwasher, dug out my price guides and reference books. When I went into the living room, the contents of the boxes were strewn on the floor. One glance and I knew Roxanne's immediate problems could be solved. Steve sat with a Mettlach stein in his hand, hefting it and admiring the design. I gave Roxanne a note pad and a pen.

"You write. Steve, look at the bottom of everything and call. Give me any numbers you see. Me, I search."

He turned the stein over. "There's a castle sort of thing. Number two-oh-two-four."

"Two-oh-two-four? Half liter. Shield of Berlin. Four hundred and ninety-five dollars."

"What?" They both reacted at once. Roxanne grabbed the stein from Steve. "For this?" Her voice rose with disbelief.

I tucked my finger in the book to keep my place.

"Before we get too excited," I said, "that's only the price listed. You're not going to get it. Even antique dealers don't expect to get it. Unless they have a collector who wants it very badly."

"There are eight of them." Roxanne was awestruck.

"Start writing."

Two hours later, Roxanne totaled the figures I had given her. She frowned and added once more.

"Twenty-six-thousand, four hundred and ten." She looked up at me, wide-eyed. "Is that possible?"

"That's only an approximation. Some of this stuff isn't listed. I put a value according to an equivalent piece. The total could be a couple of thousand more or less. I'm not an expert. But I'd guess somewhere between twenty and thirty."

"Thousand?" Steve whistled. "Who the hell's going to pay her thirty thousand dollars for this junk?"

"Nobody." Roxanne's face fell and I continued. "Hey. You'll make money on it, but nowhere near thirty thousand dollars. Let's get real here. There are three ways you can flog this stuff. You can put ads in the papers and hope collectors will spot them and call. That way, you'll get closest to top dollar. But you'll spend money you haven't got and it'll take time. Or you can trot around to one antique dealer after another, sell a piece here, a piece there. Or you can offer the lot to a single dealer."

"What do you think I should do?"

"Offer the works to a single dealer. You need the money right now."

"How much do you think I'll get?"

"I'd guess maybe ten. Ten thousand. At the outside."

"But if it's worth—"

"If you have a place to display it. If you have access to people who want to buy. If you can afford to wait a month, a year, even longer, for the buyer to find you. Face it, no antique dealer is going to pay you a hundred bucks for something he can't sell for more than a hundred bucks. He has to make a living, too."

Roxanne nodded, her face rueful. "I guess. How do I find a dealer?"

"Charles Harwood. You spoke to him the other day."

"Would you call him?"

I glanced at my watch. "He's probably at the shop."

He answered on the second ring. "This is Canterbury House. Charles Harwood here." His accent was pure Rich Little doing Prince Charles. "May I help you?"

"Hi, Charlie. It's Catherine."

"Hey, Kitty Cat." His voice dropped to its normal pitch and inflection. "My table ready?"

"Monday. All three." I gestured at Roxanne for the list. "I want to run something past you. Clarice Cliff. Paul Ysart. Rolex. Mettlach. Quimper. Mary Gregory. Lalique. A Tiffany bronze paperweight. Jewelry, including quite a lot of marcasite on sterling. Art deco this and that. Several old Mucha posters. And a signed Daum *pâté-de-verre* I can't track down but think it has to be choice. Interested?"

There was a heartbeat's silence. When he spoke, his voice had sharpened. "Have you called anyone else?"

"You first. Want to come by tomorrow? Or maybe Monday?"

"Hold it a second." I could hear muffled words, then he was back. "Cat? We're closing in twenty minutes. How about we pick up Chinese and come straight out? Should take us about an hour."

"Great. Pick up for six. I'll pay the difference."

"If you've got what you say, it's on the house. Lock the door. Draw the blinds. And stay off the bleeding phone. We'll be there in an hour at the outside." He hung up.

"So quickly?" Roxanne was startled when I relayed the conversation.

"You don't sit on your thumbs in Charlie's world. There's a dwindling supply of antiques to be found and the competition for them is lethal." I frowned at the hodge-podge on the living-room floor. "Let's get this stuff looking good. Steve, there're some of my old flea-market folding tables in the basement. Roxanne, go get a couple of sheets out of the linen closet."

While we worked, I prepared Roxanne for Charles Har-wood and Rafael Verdoni. Particularly for Rafael.

Charlie is fifty-eight years old. He's six-feet-two and he still has the build of a professional athlete. Which he could easily have become. He had played college football well enough to catch the eye of pro scouts, had boxed, had made the Olympic swimming team. He had spent most of his adult life denying his homosexuality, had ventured a brief and bitter marriage and at age forty-six, a salesman in his family's printing house, had prepared himself to spend the rest of his life alone.

One hot August night, returning from his parents' summer home, he stopped off at a roadside bar for a sandwich and a beer, planning to wait out the Sunday traffic streaming back into the city. At the next table, a group of men were giving the waiter a hard time. The waiter was in his mid-twenties and patently gay. As the taunts became more abusive, Charles rose to leave.

"Then one of those redneck bastards said something like *'You got anything down here, girlie,'* and grabbed Rafe's genitals and twisted. Hard." Charlie had told me the story. "Something snapped inside my head. The first time in my life I did something without considering the consequences. Without thinking *how the hell is this going to affect the family.* I went berserk."

By the time I met them, Charlie and Rafe had been together five years and there was nothing left of the printing salesman or the waiter. They were Canterbury House Antiques, expensive, exclusive and authoritative. Charlie, with a flair for show he had been unaware of, had created Charles Harwood.

A black patch covered the empty socket of the left eye he had lost in the fight to save Rafe. The remaining hazel eye was so pale it resembled the wicked yellow eye of a lion. A precisely trimmed salt-and-pepper Vandyke beard hid his misshapen jaw.

He had designed a wardrobe, faintly Edwardian, exclusively in black, worn with white silk turtleneck jerseys, always with a fresh red rosebud in his buttonhole. The sheer size of him, the immaculate grooming and that one fierce, golden eye made him an intimidating public presence. In private, he was as warm and bustling and bossy as a Jewish mother.

Rafe had been savagely beaten, dragged unconscious across a cinder parking lot and thrown into a drainage ditch. Charlie, half blind, his shattered jaw hanging, three broken ribs making every breath agony, had crawled until he found Rafe and held him in his arms until an ambulance arrived.

I met Rafe for the first time in the cluttered workroom hidden behind the muted elegance of Canterbury House.

He stood in front of a massively gilt-framed old oil painting, searching for a signature. A sunbeam had found its way through the window and fixed on him, spotlighting him in profile against the gloom of a dark and murky landscape. He wore a pale ivory silk shirt and narrow brown velour trousers and had unconsciously struck a graceful pose, fist on hip, long legs apart, one booted foot placed ahead of the other. His head in profile was pure David, and beautiful. Aquiline nose, full curved mouth, black curly hair with a dusting of white at the temple.

I stood motionless, entranced by the theatrical effect of light and shadow.

He became aware of my presence and turned to face me. The sunbeam that had been so magical turned cruel, highlighting the ruin of the left side of his face.

The skin from his temple to his jaw was deeply pitted, the eyebrow gone, the eyelid drawn down at the corner by a scar curving from the hairline to a drooping upper lip. Above his lobeless ear was a mass of scar tissue, dead white in the pitiless light. Only his eyes—his dark eyes—were amused at what had to be an expression of shock on my face.

"It's okay." Rafe's smile was one-sided. The left side of his face was frozen, immobile. His damaged voice was soft and rusty. "You'll get used to it. Didn't Charlie, that sonovabitch, warn you?"

They arrived within the hour, arms laden with white cardboard takeout cartons.

"Point me at the kitchen. Fast," Charlie barked. "I've got a goddamn box leaking hot plum sauce into my crotch."

He bolted for the kitchen. Rafe followed, grinning.

"It isn't the family jewels you're worried about. It's those four-hundred-dollar fancy pants," he chortled.

"At sixty bucks a whack to have them cleaned? You're damn well right," Charlie snarled. "Steve? Here. Take this crap. Where's the bleeding bathroom?"

He disappeared down the hall, passing Brandy loping toward the kitchen with ears erect, *what am I missing?* Trailing her was Cassie, rumpled and rosy with sleep. Brandy trotted immediately to Rafe, sniffing the unfamiliar legs. Cassie stopped in the doorway. Her eyes widened. Rafe spoke first. It was a ploy he used when confronting unwitting strangers.

"Hello, sugar plum," he said. "Who are you?"

"I'm Cassie." She tilted her head. "Who are you?"

"I'm your fairy godfather." Rafe placed his cartons on the counter, treading with deliberation on Steve's foot.

Steve turned his snort of laughter into a cough. "My name is Rafael. You can call me Rafe."

Cassie looked up at him dubiously. "I never heard of fairy godfathers," she said.

"How could you?" Rafe smiled. "I'm the first one ever."

"The first one ever what?" Charlie bustled into the kitchen, a bath towel wrapped around his middle, bright red jockey shorts in one hand, his black leather trousers in the other. "Cat, have you got a sponge? Maybe if I get the sauce out of the damn pants right away. The first ever what?"

"Charlie," I jumped in. "This is Roxanne. Rafe. Roxanne. And Cassie. Okay. You want a sponge."

"Please. Hi, Roxanne." Charlie took possession of the sink, filling it with warm water and throwing directions over his shoulder. "Turn the oven on, Steve. Set it at two fifty, enough to keep the food warm." He scooped Cassie up and set her on the drain board. "Hi, sweetie. How'd you like to help me wash my panties? Rafe, go look at the stuff."

Roxanne, looking slightly dazed, offered to sponge Charlie's pants for him. "You can go with Rafe."

"*Moi?*" Charlie smiled his big white smile. "Honey, I'm just the window dressing. If we went by what I know, we'd be running a secondhand store. Cat, would you put the food in the oven and set the table? It won't take Rafe long and I'm starving."

17

"Okay." Rafe set his chopsticks down and pushed his plate away. "Enough chatter. Let's get down to business."

He set his elbows on the table, placed his palms together and tapped his index fingers.

"First the bad news. Clarice Cliff. The Fantasque coffee set has only five cups and one has a chip. We'll have to sell it with four cups. One of the Bizarre vases has a chip. The other Cliffs are fine. The Rolex watch is eighteen karat but the strap isn't original and it's gold filled. All the Mettlachs are okay except for a chip in the base of the Heidelberg. There's a crack in the pewter top of one of the others. The Lalique clock doesn't work and the hour hand is missing. Everything else is in good condition."

He paused and looked at us, one after the other. "Everybody with me so far?"

We all nodded on cue and he continued.

"The good news." He smiled his one-sided smile. "You were right about the Daum, Cat. It's a fine piece. It's going to take a bit of research, but I have a feeling it's way up there."

"Way up where?" I glanced at Roxanne. Her face was calm, but her hands were tight fists. "Come on, Rafe. Let's go right to the bottom line."

"Sure." He had followed my eyes, noted the white knuckles. "Here's the deal. For everything but the Daum, nine thousand. Two thousand in cash here and now. A check for seven thousand dated Monday." He leaned back and waited.

Roxanne looked across at me, her eyes questioning. I nodded and she smiled, letting out her pent-up breath.

"Okay." Rafe nodded. "Now. The Daum. I'd like to take it on consignment. Twenty-five percent for us when it sells, the rest for you."

"Consignment?" Charlie howled. "I thought we agreed. No more bleeding consignment."

"On consignment," Rafe stated firmly. "Because I don't know enough about it. And because it could be worth twenty thousand or more. We don't want to lay out that kind of money right now, and you know damn well Max would give his eyeteeth to get his hands on it."

"Screw Max," Charlie roared. "And screw you, too, you twit. Why the hell don't you tell Roxanne the damn thing's only worth five hundred bucks? She'd be ignorantly blissful with that." His yellow eye glinted at Roxanne. "Wouldn't you, dear heart?"

Roxanne nodded, laughing.

"Ignore him," Rafe husked at Roxanne. "He thinks the eye patch entitles him to behave like a pirate."

"Bugger you, me darlin' two-faced jerk." Charlie slapped Rafe's scarred cheek affectionately. "You're too bleeding honest. We ain't never gonna get rich this way."

They left, Charlie promising to return my bath towel when they picked up their tables on Monday. I returned to the kitchen.

Roxanne had made a fresh pot of coffee. I began to pour a cup, changed my mind and sat down at the table, suddenly utterly exhausted.

"I'm going to a country fair tomorrow for background on a chapter I'm working on," Steve said. "How'd the three of you like to come along? Cassie? Would you like to go on a Ferris wheel?"

"I think so." Cassie looked up from the floor where she was feeding the remaining pork balls to Brandy. "What's a fairs wheel?"

"For Ferris wheels, showing is better than telling. How about it? Roxanne? Cat?"

"Include me out." I waved my hand. "I told Charlie he'd have his three pieces Monday. I'll have to work on them tomorrow."

"Roxanne?"

"Thanks, Steve. I'll stay and help Catherine."

"Please," I protested. "Go. Cassie'll love it. Besides, I work better by myself."

Which was the truth, but not all of it. I just wanted to be alone again for a while.

"Hey, Cat," Steve called as I was leaving the kitchen. "It just occurred to me. Who do you think the black Jag was?"

A chill slid down my spine.

I shrugged. "You were probably right. Some real-estate character. Who else?"

18

*W*orking on the patio, I could almost believe the events of the past two weeks were a particularly vivid nightmare.

Great, knobby cotton-wool clouds metamorphosed and drifted across a sky of intense summer blue. The ineffably sweet strains of Mendelssohn's violin concerto poured from the house, soaring into the limpid, lilac-scented air.

Brandy sprawled dreaming in the dappled shade of the oak tree, chest heaving, paws twitching, in happy pursuit of ghostly squirrels. A dragonfly, iridescently blue, hovered for a brief inspection, then skittered away, panicked by the sudden flick of a plumed tail.

I paused and closed my eyes, letting the timeless serenity of the concerto's andante movement flow over me.

Everything's going to be okay.

My house is safe. I can step up my pace, double or triple my output to meet expenses. I'll go after every dealer in town, even that idiot interior decorator who wanted me to strip the blue paint off an eighteenth-century pine armoire.

I'll psych myself into believing Laurie and Andy are three hundred miles away, healthy and happy and too busy to visit. It's going to be all right. It's going to be okay.

I should have known better.

19

$\mathscr{I}$woke in the morning to silence and the smell of coffee. Roxanne had left a note on the kitchen table.

> *Didn't want to wake you. The police phoned. Asked me to come down to the station. Very polite. Said it shouldn't take long. I don't think we should start worrying. Made fresh coffee. See you soon.*
> *P.S. Taking Brandy with us.*

I was pouring coffee when I heard the front door fly open. Cassie and Brandy raced into the kitchen.

"Hi, Auntie Cat!" Cassie plunked herself into a chair and placed her elbows on the table. Brandy headed for her water bowl. "Guess where we were!"

"Auntie Cat? Whatever happened to Aunt Catherine?"

"Steve said an Aunt Catherine has . . ." She pursed her pink mouth and frowned. "Steve said—"

"Steve said Aunt Catherines have blue hair and fat ankles." Roxanne came into the kitchen carrying a paper grocery bag.

Cassie nodded. "Steve said if I didn't call you Auntie Cat, you'd get them too. Didn't he, Mummy?"

"Steve is a nut." Roxanne set the bag on the counter. "I picked up milk and eggs," she said. "How would you two like French toast for breakfast?"

"Great." I took my coffee cup and sat down at the table beside Cassie. "So? Did you like the Ferris wheel?"

She shook her head vigorously, her ponytail whipping around her cheeks. "Not very. I like the horsies on the merry-go-round better."

"Cassie." Roxanne carried her coffee to the table and sat down opposite me. "Why don't you and Brandy go outside and play? Cat and I have to talk."

"Can't I talk too?"

"No. You can listen all you want. But you can't talk. Not one word."

Cassie thought about it, then slid from the chair.

"I'll call you when breakfast is ready," Roxanne promised.

We watched Cassie and Brandy race to the cedar hedge, turn and race back. Cassie flopped on the grass, her arms spread wide. Brandy, tail sweeping, licked her flushed face.

"The police had us there to identify a suspect." Roxanne's eyes smiled at Cassie's squeals of delight.

"Us?"

"The tellers. The black woman. An elderly couple." She turned her attention to me. "A shopkeeper from the mall. Two women, I think they're mother and daughter. An old man. An older woman. They're all convinced it was a man dressed up as a woman."

"What about the suspect? Did anyone identify him?"

Roxanne shook her head. "No. He was too tall. Or too short. Half of them thought he was too fat. The others thought he was too thin. Wrong voice. The only agreement was on the dress. And the canvas bag. Everybody remembered the bag was bright yellow. Oh, and the black woman remembered that the rims on the glasses were red. Where did you put the stuff?"

"Under my bed. I'll get rid of it."

"The dress for sure." She set her coffee cup down and leaned on her elbows. "I'm going to deposit Charlie's check. Then Cassie and I are going shopping for a red tricycle. Do you think that's extravagant?"

"Extravagant? A tricycle?"

"Wayne said tricycles are a waste of money. Cassie'd only outgrow it."

"Oh, for God's sake," I said in disgust. "Listen, Roxanne. As of now, stop thinking about what Wayne said or did. Close that door. Lock it. Throw away the key. Forget there ever was a Wayne."

Roxanne stared down into her empty cup. "Is that what you did?" she finally asked.

"No. I wasn't that smart. But it's how you survive. You don't let them have any more of your life than you've already given them."

"You make it sound easy."

"I didn't say it was easy." I shrugged. "It isn't easy. But you learn from it. And the most valuable lesson you'll learn is that the past exists only in your head. It isn't here. It isn't now. It's gone and finished. It's garbage. You can either walk away from it with what you learned or you can carry it on your back and let it ruin the rest of your life." I stopped abruptly and smiled at her. "End of lecture. Tell me, did you have a good time yesterday?"

Roxanne's eyes flew up to mine, startled. "Yesterday? Yes. As a matter of fact, I did."

"What do you think of Steve?"

Roxanne lifted her shoulders. Her eyes were amused. "Steve? He's nice."

I waited. She didn't continue. "But?"

Roxanne laughed. "Have you ever seen two cats circling each other? They want to be friends, but they're not sure what breed of cat they're dealing with? That's what we're like."

"Gun-shy. Both of you."

"I guess. Thank goodness for Cassie. She filled in all the gaps. She's crazy about him." Roxanne picked up her cup and carried it to the sink. She broke four eggs into a bowl, then paused, her hands placed flat on the counter.

"Cat? If I ask you a question, would you answer truthfully? No polite bullshit. The truth?"

"Why wouldn't I? Ask."

"How fast do you want us out of here?"

My face must have reflected my blank reaction. She folded her arms across her breasts, unconsciously hugging herself.

"I'm going to have to find a job. And a place to live. I know you said we should stay until Legal Aid . . . but that's not a factor anymore. I have the money from Charlie and Rafe." Roxanne drew a deep breath. "Old Chinese proverb say fish and guests stink after three days. We've been here four. Is the smell beginning to get to you?"

Her mouth was smiling. Her eyes were sending a different message. *I'm scared. I'm really scared.*

I know. I remember.

Women hiding a bad marriage don't have close friends. They have too much covering up to do, too many lies to tell. If they have any pride, if they're not whiners to begin with, they put up a good front, a false front that doesn't permit the intimacy of friendship. When they leave, unless they have the support of the right kind of family, they're alone. Alone and afraid.

The first months are pure hell. They're the walking wounded, and every day demands they make lonely decisions. A place to live. A job. A place for the children. Sending them out alone into a new and frightening world. The bewilderment on those trusting faces adding guilt to the fear and aching self-doubt.

Eventually the demoralizing fear fades. The alien apartment becomes home. The job a familiar routine. Children find new friends. Life *does* go on. Time *does* heal.

But those first months. They're killers.

"Why don't we do it this way?" I said. "First you sic a lawyer onto Wayne. For child support at least. Then you find a job. Settle into it without worrying about Cassie.

We'll hit garage sales through the summer for the things you're going to need. In the fall, you look for a place to live. A nursery school for Cassie. How's that sound?"

The smile reached her eyes. "Thank you, Cat. But I pay rent. Or half the expenses. Whichever you prefer."

I remembered my meager bank balance and resisted the impulse to tell her to forget it.

"Half the expenses?"

"Done."

Charlie and Rafe arrived at noon. I offered lunch and they accepted, with Charlie's proviso that it be a salad and that he prepare it.

"Lakeshore Drive snots." Charlie ripped lettuce leaf by leaf into a big wooden bowl. "They think their used toilet paper is worth money."

"What?" I looked at Rafe. He winked back at me.

"This stainless-steel old bitch strolls into the store and informs us she may be interested in letting us make an *offah on her fawmly traysures.*" Charlie's mimicry was wicked. "So we shlep our butts all the way out to this massive old Tudor on Lakeshore, thinking maybe we can afford to buy a couple of good pieces."

He picked up a knife and began chopping shallots.

"So the Cranberry is Flash and scratched up and down and sideways, and the sterling is plate worn to the brass. The Limoges dinner set is old, but some arsehole's been putting it in the dishwasher for thirty years. Gold's long gone. Chips and cracks. Missing pieces. She'll consider accepting three thousand for the set."

"The Meissen," Rafe prompted.

"Ah yes. The Meissen," Charlie intoned. "Broken blossoms and headless cherubs. Fingerless ladies with dark brown glue rings around their necks. And the old bitch implies we're fortunate to have the opportunity to bid on them. Bid, for Christ's sake. Who the hell would bid on that crap?"

"Give her Max's number," I volunteered.

Rafe laughed. Charlie smacked the countertop with the flat of the knife. "*Merde*," he said. "Why didn't I think of that?"

"So you didn't get anything?"

"The hell we didn't." Charlie's yellow eye glinted. "A pair of old Nippon moriage vases yay high." He held the knife blade two feet above the counter. "Thirty bucks the pair."

"*Thirty?* For Nippon? How?"

"My sly friend there." Charlie waved the knife at Rafe. "He picks up one of the vases. Turns it over. Disappointed. Says, 'Oh, it's Japan.'"

"Aw, Rafe." I smiled across the table at him. "And I always thought you were the honest one."

Rafe shrugged. "Did I lie? Nippon is Japan. And the woman was happy as a pig in shit. She thought she was really putting one over on us, getting thirty dollars for a lousy pair of 'Made-in-Japan' vases."

"At least this once we'll cover our time and gas." Charlie added diced green peppers and sliced cucumbers to the salad. "Got any chichi peas?"

"In the cupboard to your right. Hasn't picking been any good lately?"

"Lot of empty trips." Rafe shook his head, then added almost too casually, "Tell me about Roxanne."

"Roxanne? Why?"

"Just curious."

"Sure you are." I caught the look that passed between them. While we ate, I told Charlie and Rafe about Roxanne, omitting the details of how we had taken possession of her inheritance.

When I finished, Rafe nodded an *I told you so* at Charlie. Charlie spread his hands wide in a gesture of surrender.

I looked from one to the other. "What?"

"We had an argument over the consignment." Charlie's one golden eye was without its normal glint of humor. "I thought she might be one of the clucks we get selling off Granny's old goodies to finance some asshole whim like a tit implant. I don't feel under any obligation to finance their silly lives."

"In other words, you were going to stiff her. Roxanne."

The twinkle returned. "Hey, I was gonna try."

Rafe snorted. "Come on, Charlie. Actually, he thought she might have more to sell. I knew she didn't."

"You were right. Nothing. Nada. Literally."

"Then we've got good news for her."

"The Daum?"

Rafe nodded. "Eighteen thousand. We've got a buyer. He'll knock us down to sixteen. Four to us, twelve to her."

"*Twelve thousand?* Fantastic. When?"

"A week, ten days." Rafe glanced at his watch. "Cat, I hate to eat and run, but we've got to get back to the shop. Is my table ready?"

"In the basement. All three."

We each carried a piece out to their van. Rafe opened the rear doors and pushed aside a painted bowfront chest of drawers to make space for the tables.

"Cat?" Charlie gestured at the chest. "I know you hate to strip white paint, but do you want to take a stab at this? Rafe thinks it's rosewood. Nice bonnet drawer too."

"Yeah, sure." White paint. Yuk. "Let's take it back to the patio. I'll start on it today."

I waved goodbye and went down to the basement to collect the stripping gear. The doorbell rang and I ran back up the stairs, wondering what they had forgotten.

I opened the front door and my mouth went dry.

A black car was idling in the driveway. Leaning against

the trunk, arms folded across a massive chest, was a monster in a gray-silk suit and black wraparound sunglasses.

I could hear the blood rushing in my ears. I swear I felt a click as my eyes refocused to take in the figure framed in the doorway.

Black-glass stare. Purple mouth.

Liverlips.

20

Without taking his eyes from my face, he raised his arm. He snapped his fingers.

The Hulk in the shiny suit lifted the trunk lid. He reached down in the trunk and brought out a yellow canvas bag. My yellow canvas bag.

Suddenly my skin was too tight.

He dipped into the bag, lifted out the garish dress. Held it up for me to see. Let it drop back into the trunk. Then the wig. The shoes. The glasses.

He flipped the canvas bag into the trunk. Closed the lid. It caught with an expensive click.

I turned and ran.

In my bedroom, I dropped to my knees beside the bed, threw back the spread. Nothing. No yellow bag. Nothing but dust bunnies.

When? I hadn't been out of the house since . . . since Saturday morning. While I was breaking and entering, I had been broken and entered.

I pushed myself to my feet and returned to the front door. They were still there. The black car. The Hulk. And Liverlips.

"How did you get into my house?"

The purple mouth stretched into a parody of a smile. The eyes didn't change. He reached into his pocket, withdrew an envelope, thrust it at me. His silence was unnerving. My hand shook as I took the envelope from him.

Pictures. A photo of me carrying a box down the steps of Roxanne's house. Of Roxanne and Steve maneuvering the desk into Steve's van. Of Steve handing a carton to Roxanne, me visible inside the van. There were perhaps a dozen in all, each one more damning than the last. I went through them twice, trying to get control over the quivering that extended from my knees to my throat. I gritted my teeth and looked back up into those shiny, impenetrable eyes.

"Who are you? What do you want?"

He shrugged. "What matters is I know who you are. You and me need to talk." His voice, as reedy and shallow as a boy's, dissipated the aura of menace his silence had created. "So, Catherine. You going to invite me in? Or do we talk here?"

"My name is Mrs. Wilde." The intimacy of my given name on those lips made my skin crawl. "You can talk here."

There was the merest flicker in the black eyes. He shrugged again. "Whatever."

"What do you want?"

"First we talk about what you don't want. You don't want what I've got getting to the police."

I thrust the pictures at him. "These pictures don't mean a thing. That's her house. Those are her belongings."

"Who you kidding?" He ignored the pictures. "Don't fuck me around, Catherine."

My momentary bravado collapsed. I pushed the pictures into my shirt pocket with a hand that shook.

"What do you want?"

"I want you to clean an apartment. Tomorrow."

"What?"

"You're going to clean an apartment. Tomorrow morning. Make like a cleaning woman."

A cleaning woman? My first impulse was to laugh. My face must have mirrored the impulse. His eyes turned flat and narrow, and suddenly the menace was real. I said nothing.

"There's an espresso bar on the corner of Barclay and Sixth. Downtown. Be there at ten to nine. Tomorrow morning." He ran his lizard eyes up and down, taking in the sneakers, the jeans, the cotton shirt. "You can wear what you got on."

He turned away. At the car door, he paused. "Be there." The reedy voice was hard. "You fuck with me, Catherine, and all that crap gets turned over to a friend. A cop friend. Count on it."

The black car peeled away, leaving me on the front steps as confused as I've ever been in my life. And frightened.

Five minutes later, a taxi pulled up. Brandy scrambled out, huffy over sharing the rear seat with a red tricycle, Cassie and Roxanne.

Roxanne paid the driver, her face glum.

"What happened? Where's your car?"

"She died." Roxanne expelled an angry breath. "She coughed. She shuddered. She died, dammit."

"I'm not surprised. The only thing holding that car together was the dirt. Relax, Roxanne. You're going to be rich next week."

Roxanne's face lit up. "I am?"

"Twelve thousand dollars. That's the good news."

21

"Clean an apartment?" Roxanne riffled through the photos again. "I don't get it."

We were on the patio. Cassie pedaled past, lap seven in her circuit tour of the paved walk circling the house. Brandy loped easily alongside, pacing her.

"Look at me, Mummy!" Cassie cried. "Watch me!"

"We're watching, honey," Roxanne called. "You're terrific."

Cassie disappeared around the corner of the house. Roxanne dropped the pictures on the table, shaking her head.

"Who is this guy?"

"Remember when we were running out of the bank? A man at the door? Coming in?"

"Cat, believe me, I didn't see anything from the moment you yelled *freeze* till you showed me that damn knife in the parking lot."

"That was him. I think he followed us from the bank to the school parking lot. I think he got my car license number when I stripped the tape off the plate. And I think he's been following me since." I told her about the black car.

"You didn't tell me any of this."

"I wasn't sure until I saw the car today. It's the same black car."

"The car Steve saw?"

I nodded. "He must have followed us there on Saturday, come back here, broken into the house, found the stuff under the bed, gone back to your place and taken the pictures."

Roxanne chewed her lower lip, frowning. "Cat," she said. "You know and I know there has to be more to it than cleaning an apartment. All that to get a cleaning woman?"

"I've been thinking the same thing."

"We should call the police." She grimaced. "We can't call the police."

"Not hardly," I agreed.

"Who is this creep? What does he want? Have you any idea what it's all about?"

"Not a clue. All I know is, he scares me. And the gorilla with him? He's really scary."

"So what are we going to do?"

"We don't have much in the way of options. I guess I clean. And hope that if whatever it is I'm doing is illegal, I don't get caught doing it."

22

*T*ony's Espresso Bar was a narrow, chrome-and-mirror cave redolent with the odor of coffee and the yeasty scent of warm bread. Elevator music oozed around the buzz of conversation, carried on by people I couldn't see until my eyes adjusted from the bright morning sunshine outside.

The place was full of business people, mostly men in light summer suits, catching a fast breakfast. A counter on the right was doing a brisk takeout business. Along the left wall was a row of booths, all occupied. Halfway down was Liverlips, his eyes on me, his face expressionless, holding a cup with both hands.

He jerked his head sideways as I reached the table. Across from him, the Hulk, eyes hidden behind dark glasses, slid closer to the wall, making room on the bench for me.

"Sit," Liverlips ordered.

I sat. Liverlips waved the approaching waiter away.

"The apartment building on the corner." He reached in his pocket, dropped a key ring on the table. "The Twenty-one Hundred. You go to six-twelve." He pushed the key ring at me. "One key is for the lobby, the other for the apartment. You go in. You clean the place. You get out before twelve."

"When do I get my clothes back? And the negatives."

He gave me that flat, obsidian stare. "You clean the place like it's what you do, understand? No half-assed job. And you get out before twelve noon. Understand?"

I nodded. "When do I get my clothes back?"

He withdrew a black box from his pocket and set it on the table. "When you do the bedroom, you put this under the mattress. Between the mattress and the box spring."

He pushed the box across the table. It was the size and shape of an eight-track tape cassette, with a shallow dome. "What is it?" I asked.

He glared. "It's a tape recorder, stupid. It's voice activated and right now it's wasting tape on this asshole conversation. So shut up and listen. You put it between the mattress and the box spring. Got that? Then you make the bed like it's supposed to be made. Got that? Now, beat it."

I stared down at the tape recorder. At the keys. I tightened my grip on my handbag. "When do I get my clothes back?"

He brought his fist down on the table. Hard. My heart leaped at the sudden crash. Beside me, the Hulk began a slow, deliberate slide, forcing me from the bench. Liverlips raised his hand and the pressure ceased.

"Listen, you mangy old cunt." His voice rose to a fluty snarl. His eyes glittered, the black irises like jet beads on a field of snow. He leaned across the table. "Take the keys and get your fat ass out of here. Do what I told you, like I told you. Exactly like I told you. Now fuck off."

I picked up the recorder and keys with hands that trembled. I walked the length of the room on legs that shook, my stomach quivering with outrage and genuine fear. Stepping out from the cafe, I was blinded by the brilliance of sunlight pouring down on the real world outside. I waited for the green light and crossed the street.

I do not have a fat ass.

23

$\mathcal{T}$wenty-one Hundred Barclay is an apartment building on a street of apartment buildings, all with shops on ground level, all with names borrowed from *Burke's Peerage*. "Duke of Kent" is lettered in gold on glass lobby doors set back between a florist's shop on the left and a real estate office on the right.

I checked the tenants' listing in the foyer. Six-twelve was S. *Starr*. The first key I tried opened the door to the inside lobby. Marble floor. Two totally forgettable pictures hung above two pale green, fake-leather couches. Two mirrored elevator doors flanked by two tall plastic cedar trees. Spotlights recessed in an egg-crate plastic ceiling. Clean, quiet and safe. Not one thing any self-respecting thief would consider stealing.

The elevator was an upright box lined with padded maroon plastic grained to imitate leather. It rose silently, the coin light above the door slipping from one to six.

Six-twelve was the first apartment to the left of the glass-brick wall facing the elevators. The second key opened the lock and I stepped into what Charlie, needling Rafe, called a wop's wet dream.

"Up yours, Charlie." Rafe had lifted a lazy finger. "Wops were making beautiful things a thousand years before your bog-trotting ancestors figured out how to produce a clay pisspot."

It was all there. Plush rugs, pale blue. Flocked wallpaper, burgundy and gold. Balloon sheers at the windows behind burgundy velvet drapes held back by gilt cupids in mid flight. Between the windows, a two-foot alabaster Venus on the half shell, mounted on a three-foot gilded column. Oval tables of marble resting on the shoulders of golden cherubs. Ornate Capo di Monte lamps with swagged and fringed silk shades. An eight-foot sofa of carved, curved wood, gilt-brushed, framing burgundy and blue cut-velvet upholstery. A gold-veined mirror, gilt-framed, above a fake fireplace of marble and gilded metal roses. A dining area of white and gold, dominated by an enormous gold chandelier dripping crystals and blue porcelain roses.

And bibelots everywhere, on every surface.

Shepherdesses with downcast eyes and golden crooks. Fragile ladies in billowing skirts casting coy smiles at bewigged dandies in floral waistcoats and buckled shoes. Overblown ceramic roses in woven ceramic baskets. Gilded Venetian-glass bonbon bowls. On the mantel, a truly hideous clock of filigreed brass, scabrous with pink porcelain roses.

A cleaning woman's nightmare.

The kitchen was as stark as the living room was opulent, a monument to melamine in black and white.

Centered precisely on a black plastic place mat on a white melamine table were two twenty-dollar bills and a note.

> *Mrs. Karpinka:*
> *Please clean out the fridge today. A bottle of*
> *daiquiri mix got spilled and it's all under the*
> *veggie bins. Leave the laundry till Friday if you*
> *have to.*
> *Stella S.*

Stella S. Stella Starr. For a fleeting moment, the name seemed familiar. I shook my head. I wouldn't forget anybody named Stella Starr.

It took me five minutes to locate all the cleaning supplies

I would require. I loaded the soiled black melamine dishes from the sink to the dishwasher, threw dried pizza crusts, the empty bottle of daiquiri mix and the wilted remains of a salad into the garbage, then opened the fridge door. Half a dozen eggs. Two tired carrots. A container of soured cottage cheese. A half bottle of white wine.

Out of curiosity, I checked the cupboards. A jar of instant coffee. Two cans of chicken soup. A bottle of soy sauce.

Whoever Stella Starr was, she was not a cook.

I finished cleaning the kitchen. Vacuumed and dusted the living room. Then waded into the bathroom.

Wet towels on the floor. Strands of black hair and green blobs of toothpaste in the sink. Beige rings left by a foundation bottle cap on the water-stained countertop. A cracked plastic eyeshadow palette bleeding mauve powder. A makeup brush and a dirty comb stuck upright in the scummy tooth glass. Spattered mirror. A pink wicker wastebasket overflowing with lipsticked tissues, soiled cotton balls, torn panty hose and crumpled drugstore bags. Toilet left unflushed. A pair of stained panties and a safety-pinned bra in the gray-ringed bathtub.

Stella Starr was a slob.

The bedroom was a mess of discarded clothes and shoes and lingerie. A purple quilted-velvet bedspread lay in a heap on the lavender rug beside a queen-sized canopy bed. A leggy porcelain doll dressed in purple lace lay sprawled on the wrinkled lavender satin sheets. I waded in.

Mrs. Karpinka, if she did the laundry as well, was vastly underpaid.

On the night table, under a sheer mauve nightgown, I found a silver-framed photo after the Las Vegas night-club school. A blue-eyed, black-haired woman in a deep-cut purple dress, trying hard to look like Elizabeth Taylor, cheek to cheek with a white-haired man, each with a broad white smile.

Stella Starr had to be in her forties. The man was older. Dark eyes, heavy black brows, prominent nose, deep tan doing its best to belie sixty. A lean and feral sixty.

Stripping the bed, I caught movement out of the corner of my eye. I froze, heart thumping. I looked cautiously around, over my shoulder, then up.

The underpart of the canopy was a huge mirror. My first reaction was prudish shock. Then I giggled. I can't imagine a bigger turnoff than lying prone watching the reflection of a sixty-year-old butt, no matter how well preserved, humping. Maybe Stella Starr was nearsighted.

Grinning to myself, I put the soiled sheets in the hamper in the bathroom, found fresh ones in a hall closet. Then I went to the kitchen for the tape recorder.

The floral clock began a ponderous striking. I glanced at my watch, suddenly panicked. Twelve o'clock.

I ran to the bedroom, made up the bed, slid the cassette in place between the box spring and the mattress, raced to the kitchen, snatched up the bills and my bag. At eight minutes past twelve, I stepped out of the apartment, scrabbling in my pocket for the key to lock the door behind me.

The elevator door slid open as I locked the door. The man in the silver frame stepped from the cage into the brightness streaming from the glass-brick wall. I dropped the keys out of sheer fright. I bent to retrieve them, dumping half the contents of my handbag onto the floor.

"Take it easy, my friend." Mellifluous. A deep, molten-honey voice. "You don't have to be in such a rush. I don't mind holding the elevator."

I thrust my wallet back in my bag and stood up.

He smiled, his teeth glistening in the deeply tanned face, his eyes liquid chocolate.

Once, in New York, I watched as Caesar Romero swept into the lobby of the Algonquin Hotel. He had to be close to sixty then. His hair was white, his face mahogany. A camel-hair coat slung over his shoulders flared behind him like a cape. For two heartbeats, everyone in that jaded place paused. And looked. This man had that same indefinable quality, that same presence. I was acutely aware of him as I stepped past him into the elevator.

I turned to face him. He let his hand drop when I pressed the *down* button.

"Thank you."

His smile deepened. "It was my pleasure."

I don't know where the words came from. I don't know what made me say them. Perhaps I felt a sense of revulsion at the thought of Liverlips eavesdropping on this elegant man's pillow talk.

"Get out of here," I said, and added the first words that came to mind. "The place is on fire."

The smile vanished. His eyes narrowed and turned to ice, then the door slid closed and the elevator began its descent.

The place is on fire? Where had *that* come from?

There was no sign of Liverlips or the Hulk in the espresso bar on the corner.

24

*C*assie was napping when I reached home.

"She was hot and cranky." Roxanne set out a sandwich for me. "Riding that damn trike all morning in this heat. Even Brandy had the sense to head for the basement." She brought two glasses of iced tea and settled into the chair across from me. "Okay."

She listened without comment, amused by the mirrored canopy, wrinkling her nose when I described the state of Stella Starr's bathroom, intrigued by the man in the silver frame. She shook her head when I finished.

"Does it make any sense to you?" she asked. "Who are these people? Why a bug? And why you?"

"Who knows? Maybe Stella Starr belongs to Liverlips and he thinks she's fooling around? Maybe Liverlips is trying to get something on the old man? Who cares? What worries me is that he still has my clothes and the pictures. What worries me is maybe having to go through the whole damn routine again to retrieve the cassette."

She grinned. "Hey. You made forty bucks."

"And earned every penny." The phone rang and I reached for it. "Stella Starr's a *schmutz*. Hello?"

"Who's Stella Starr?" It was Charlie. "And what the hell's a *schmutz*?"

"A slattern. A sloven. A slob. Hello, Charlie."

"Hi, Cat. Listen. I've got a customer hot for the bonnet chest. I don't want to give her a chance to cool off. Can you give me an idea of how soon it'll be ready?"

"Tomorrow? If I strip it today, I can do the finish in the morning. Late tomorrow."

"Aw, Cat, you're a pussycat. Charge me overtime. We'll come by after we close, say five-thirtyish?"

"Fine. See you." I hung up. "Well, there goes the day."

"Want help?"

I shook my head. "Thanks, but we'd just get in each other's way."

Roxanne carried the soiled dishes to the sink. "I made up a grocery list. Anything special you want?"

"Nothing I can think of." I dug in my purse for my car keys and registration. "You'll need these. And money."

"Forget the money. Right now I'm richer than you are."

Fortunately, there was varnish under the white paint. Instead of cursing, I merely grumbled. Rafe was right, the chest was of fine rosewood, richly grained. I was digging gummy paint and varnish out of the carved grooves when Cassie burst from the kitchen, Brandy at her heels.

"We're home, Auntie Cat. Guess what." She threw her arms wide. "We bought a watermelon this big!"

"Yum." I held up a gloved warning hand. "Steer clear of this muck, Cass. It'll burn you." It wasn't necessary to warn Brandy. The mess was an old story to her. She circled my working area with mincing feet and distasteful side glances and flopped to the grass under the oak tree.

"Is it hot?" Cassie inched warily closer.

"No. It isn't hot. But it'll burn if you get some on your feet."

"How?" Cassie's feet stopped. She craned her head.

"There's lye or something in the stripper. And lye can burn right through your shoes if it wants to."

Cassie looked down at her sandals apprehensively. "Does it want to now?"

I nodded. "It always wants to."

"Why?"

"Why what?" Roxanne pushed through the screen door, carrying a tray. "How's it going? Can you take a break for lemonade?"

"You're psychic." I stripped off the rubber gloves. "I was just thinking how nice something cold and wet would be."

"Why, Auntie Cat?" Cassie was rooted, fearful of moving. "Why does it want to?"

"Because that's the only thing the silly stuff knows how to do." I scooped her up, sat down at the patio table and kissed the soft, damp skin of her nape.

"What are we talking about?" Roxanne slumped into a chair, stretched her legs and hiked her skirt up over her knees. "Damn, it's hot. How does macaroni salad for supper strike you?"

"I want watermelon," Cassie announced. "I don't want yukky old salad. I want watermelon for supper. Can I?"

"Sure," Roxanne agreed lazily. "Help me make yukky salad for us and you can have watermelon."

"Okay." Cassie licked condensation from her glass, working from bottom to top with a pink tongue.

Roxanne's nose wrinkled. "Cassie! *That's* yukky. Where'd you learn to do a thing like that?"

"Brandy does it," Cassie said serenely.

"Brandy's a dog. You're a people. People don't lick the outside of their glasses."

"Okay." Cassie reached into her glass and fished out an ice cube. She slipped down from my knee and went to where Brandy lay. One eye opened warily as Cassie flopped down on the grass.

"Here, Brandy." Cassie lifted Brandy's upper lip and pushed the ice between the lethal-looking teeth.

Roxanne half rose to protest and changed her mind. "The hell with it." She flapped a limp hand. "Brandy's old enough to take care of herself. How long before you're done?"

"Me? Maybe an hour."

"Good." Roxanne gathered the empty glasses. "Come on, Cassie. We'll make supper. Come on, Brandy. You can help."

I went back to work, cleaning out the jointed sections of the chest with a toothbrush dipped in turpentine. I dampened a rag with turpentine and wiped down the entire chest, ready for finishing. Three coats of paste varnish would give the wood a soft, hand-rubbed patina. The first coat could be applied after supper.

The kitchen door opened as I was stuffing a mess of paint-filled rags, gummy steel-wool pads and wads of crumpled newspaper into a garbage bag.

"Cat?"

I looked up quickly. Roxanne, her eyes too large for her face, stood in the doorway holding the screen door ajar.

"What's the matter? What's happened?"

"I . . . I turned on the radio," she said shakily. "For the news. They said . . . Cat, a bomb blew up an apartment on Barclay Street. Twenty-one-Hundred Barclay."

25

$\mathscr{T}$he six-o'clock television news report was brief.

"Police have not released the name of the victim in the explosion shortly after noon today in an apartment at Twenty-one-Hundred Barclay Street."

The announcer was replaced by a long shot of the glass lobby doors of the Duke of Kent building.

"Damage was limited mainly to the bedroom of the apartment where the explosion occurred, although windows in neighboring apartments were shattered by the blast."

The announcer reappeared. He slid a paper aside on his desk and continued, "We'll have more on that story for our eleven-o'clock newscast."

I clicked him away and glanced across at Roxanne. She was watching me with troubled eyes. I pushed myself out of my chair.

"I should put the first coat of varnish on that chest."

"I'll help," Roxanne said firmly. Not "Can I help?"

"Me too." Cassie imitated the stubborn note in Roxanne's voice.

I applied paste varnish to the drawer fronts of the chest and showed Cassie how to buff with the grain, using a soft cloth. Then I gave each of them a drawer and went to work on the chest itself. After a few moments of rubbing, Cassie looked up, frowning.

"Auntie Cat? When am I finished?"

"When it isn't tacky anymore."

"What's tacky?"

"Sticky. You rub until it isn't sticky anymore." I tested the surface of her drawer. "A little bit more."

Her enthusiasm had waned. "Do I have to?"

"No."

"Yes. You do," Roxanne said in the same tone she had used on me earlier. "You started it. You finish." She smiled at the storm clouds gathering on her daughter's face. "Why don't you sing us a song while we work?"

"Okay." Cassie smiled sunnily and launched into a chorus of *Fevver Jocka*. After *summerlama tina* Roxanne and I joined in for the *dingdangdong* ending. "Am I finished now?"

Roxanne passed a light finger over the varnish. "Just a bit more, honey."

"Okay." Cassie heaved an exaggerated sigh. "But you sing. I already did."

I cast around in my mind for a song from Laurie's childhood.

"I know one. But I'm warning you, it's sad. Are you sure you want to hear it?" I queried Roxanne with raised eyebrows.

She shrugged consent. Cassie nodded. "I like sad."

"Here goes then."

My dears don't you know, I sang, how a long time ago,
Two poor little children, whose names I don't know,
Were stolen away on a bright summer's day
And left in the woods as I've heard people say.
And when it was night, so sad was their plight,
For the sun it went down and the moon gave no light.
They sobbed and they sighed and they bitterly cried,
Then the poor little things, they lay down and died.

Cassie stopped buffing, her eyes wide. "Keep rubbing," Roxanne prompted softly.

And when they were dead, the robins so red
Brought strawberry leaves and over them spread.
And all the day long, they sang them this song.
Poor babes in the woods, poor babes in the woods.
Oh, don't you remember the babes in the woods?
Poor babes in the woods. Poor babes in the woods.

The last word hung on the air until Cassie, in a stricken voice, asked, "Did they really die?" Twenty-five years later, the same question Laurie had asked.

"I'm sorry. They really died."

"Maybe I don't like sad so much," Cassie said dubiously. "Sing it again."

I tested her drawer front. "Almost finished." I bent and kissed the top of her head. "And you've done a terrific job. How about one more minute? Then we'll go for a long drive and buy the biggest ice-cream cone we can find anywhere."

"Okay." Cassie brightened. "Sing strawberry leaves again."

"I'll sing something else." I remembered another of Laurie's favorites. I tidied up while I sang.

The horses stand around. Their feet are on the ground.
Who's going to mind the cat while I'm away, away?
Go get the ax, there's a fly on baby's chest.
Oh, a girl's best friend is her mother.
Once I lived in a lighthouse, a wild and stormy lighthouse.
Why do they build the shore so near the ocean, the ocean?
Go get the Listerine, sister wants a beau.
Oh, a girl's best friend is her mother.

Roxanne smiled. "I remember my grandmother singing that song. There have to be at least ten verses and not one of them makes sense. I used to think it was the funniest thing in the world."

Cassie was not amused. "It's dumb," she said scornfully. "I like sad better. Can we go for ice cream now?"

"Cat?" Roxanne said quietly. We'd been driving in silence for half an hour. Cassie had fallen asleep in her mother's lap. Brandy snored softly in the back. "It wasn't your fault."

"I know." The clock on the dash said ten-fifteen. I turned off Lakeshore Drive, away from the serene moon path shimmering on black water and up a street leading back to the parkway.

"They were out to kill her. One way or another. For whatever reason." Roxanne shifted to face me. Her eyes reflected the glow of the dashboard light. "Listen, Cat. I'm not saying she asked for it. Nobody asks to be killed. But what was she doing, involved with people like Liverlips? You lie down with dogs, you get up with fleas."

"Or not get up at all." I took the up ramp onto the brightly lit parkway and picked up speed. "I've been thinking about it. It may not have been her they wanted. Maybe it was him, the man in the silver frame. The man at the elevator."

"Oh." Roxanne was taken aback. "I didn't even think of him. That it could have been someone else, I mean."

"I imagine it'll be on the late news. It'll be interesting to find out just exactly who I blew away."

Roxanne was silent. I felt her eyes on me. "Cat?" she said after a moment, her voice hesitant. "You okay?"

"I'm fine. Just fine."

The newscaster switched from a prolife demonstration story to the bombing without a change in expression or tone. Behind him, a studio portrait of Stella Starr replaced the faces and placards of the milling antiabortionists.

"Stella Starr died today in a mysterious bombing at her apartment—"

"Is that her?" Roxanne asked. I nodded.

The blackened ruins of Stella's lavender bedroom filled the screen. *"Jesus Murphy,"* Roxanne breathed. The newscaster returned against a rear projection of a black-glass shop front. Lettered in gold on a display window was the name *stella starr*.

"No wonder it was familiar," I muttered.

". . . owner of the exclusive boutique." The newscaster raised bland eyes to the camera. "A spokesman for the police department stated that an early arrest is expected."

Roxanne rose abruptly. "Heard enough?"

I nodded and she cut the announcer off in mid sentence. She gazed thoughtfully at the black screen.

"How old do you think she was?" she asked.

"Fortyish." I added ten years to the portrait the television station had used. The bedside photo, unretouched, had been of a Stella with a lot more hard miles on her.

"It wasn't your fault." Roxanne crossed her arms over her breasts, hugging her elbows. "He pointed you at her. Guns don't kill, people do."

"I'm the gun?" I smiled up at her.

She grimaced. "So it's a lousy metaphor. But you know what I mean. You didn't kill her. He did."

I stood up. "I'm going to bed." I walked over to her and hugged her. She looked chilled. "It's okay, Roxanne. I'm all right. Really."

I lay sleepless, watching leafy shadows quiver on the wall while glowing numerals on the digital clock measured out the small hours of the night. I was a long way from being all right. Really.

Fifteen days ago. Daisy's phone call. Fifteen days ago, the world had lurched and sent me skittering over the edge.

The anguish of existing in a world without Laurie in it.

My baby. My friend. Never to see that elfin face again, hear her laughter. That was real.

The rage smoldering like a banked fire in the pit of my stomach when I thought of Mort. That was real.

Plotting a bank robbery had seemed as routine as preparing for a television commercial. Location. Wardrobe. Props. Timing. Casting. Lying on my familiar bed, watching the eternal moon flicker its way through the branches of the stolid old oak tree, I could almost convince myself that everything after was fantasy.

Except that a woman named Roxanne and a child named Cassie were sleeping in the next room.

And Stella Starr was dead.

Three A.M. is melodrama time. Three A.M. is when the gremlins crouch on your breast. When foreboding swells your brain until your skull is too small to contain it. Three A.M. is when the tumbrels start rolling, looming darkly in the predawn skies.

My fingerprints are everywhere in the shambles of her apartment. Liverlips has my dress and the photos. I can choose between going to prison or going bang! *whenever he points me at someone.*

I rolled over and groaned into my pillow. Chicken Little was right. *The sky is falling.*

26

"Cat? Wake up. Cat. Catherine. Wake up."

I swam groggily up out of a nightmare. I was drowning in leaden water under a pewter sky.

"Cat. Please. Wake up."

"What? What? I'm sorry," I mumbled. Sleep hadn't come until the horizon was apricot with dawn. I opened bleary eyes and focused on Roxanne, sitting on my bed, a newspaper in her hand, trouble in her eyes. "What's the matter? What time is it?"

"After nine. I'm sorry to wake you but . . ." Her hands tightened on the newspaper. "What was the cleaning woman's name? I mean the note. Do you remember the name on the note Starr left?"

"Name? Note?" I rubbed my forehead. "I don't remember. Not an ordinary name. I have to think."

"Try to remember."

I turned back the covers and swung my feet to the floor. "Give me a couple of minutes. Let me brush my teeth and throw some cold water on my face. Is there any coffee?"

"I'll make fresh."

Brushing my teeth, I studied the mirror. Were the bags under my eyes deeper and darker? The skin grayer? You look old, I accused my reflection. You are old, it replied coldly. The name on the note popped into my head. I spat, dried my face and went to the kitchen.

"Karpinka. Mrs. Karpinka."

Roxanne nodded gravely. She brought two cups of coffee to the table, set one down for me, the other for herself.

"The bomb was a pressure bomb. It was designed to go off when someone added their weight on the bed," she said. "There's a write-up on it. It also says that Stella Starr—whose real name was Staretsky, by the way—was known to the police. She was known to have connections with organized crime. The police believe her shop was a front for laundering money. They think the bombing may be a settling of accounts."

"Organized crime?" I set my cup down. "I'm a hit man for the Mafia suddenly?"

Roxanne pushed the newspaper toward me. She indicated a single paragraph halfway down the page. "Read," she said in a quiet voice.

WOMAN FOUND STRANGLED

Police are investigating the death of Mrs. Anna Karpinka of 1462 Hastings Street. Her body was found by her daughter, who had become alarmed when there was no reply to repeated phone calls. The cause of death was given as strangulation. There were no signs of forced entry. Mrs. Karpinka worked as a cleaning woman, and police are questioning her various employers as a matter of routine.

I read it twice, the chill in my stomach flowing down to my knees. I looked up at Roxanne. Her face was pale, her eyes dark and wide.

"He killed her," I said hoarsely. "He killed her for the keys. He killed her for the keys to Starr's apartment."

Roxanne nodded.

I stood up, too agitated to stay at the table. I carried my cup to the sink and looked out the window at the dark cedar hedge surrounding the yard, at the green lawn dappled in shade by the heavy foliage of the oak tree.

Cassie lay on her stomach on the patio, busily crayoning.

Brandy slept beside her, paws twitching in dreams of pursuit.

"Roxanne? I think you should take Cassie and get as far away from me as you can."

For a moment, I thought she hadn't heard me. Then she said, "You want to get rid of us?"

I swung to face her. "Of course not. You know I don't. But this thing frightens me. He frightens me."

"But it's over." Roxanne leaned forward, her expression intense. "He got what he wanted. Starr is dead. It's too bad she's dead. But if the police are right, she wasn't exactly an innocent bystander!"

"Mrs. Karpinka was."

"Maybe she wasn't."

"Roxanne. She was a cleaning woman. Do you think she'd be cleaning other people's houses if she was anything more than just a cleaning woman?"

"*I don't know!* Maybe . . ." Roxanne's shoulders lifted and fell. "I don't know. But it's *over*. You don't even have to go back for the cassette. It went boom right along with the rest of the place. It's over, Cat. Done. Finished."

"Roxanne. Think. He's killed two women. Had them killed. And if he can kill someone like Mrs. Karpinka just to get her keys, what's to stop him coming after me? Just for knowing who blew up Stella Starr?"

"But you don't know," Roxanne protested. "You don't even know his name. You don't know who he is."

"He knows who I am. He knows who I am and where I live."

"So he knows. Look. He got what he was after. Starr is gone. Kaput. He killed Karpinka to get at Starr. What does he have to gain by going after you? Even if you knew who he was, you couldn't tell anybody. He still has the clothes and the photos. He's safe and he knows it. It's over."

I shook my head. "Roxanne, one week ago, I figured I'd

rob a nice quiet little bank, pay off that son-of-a-bitch Mort and it would all be over."

"One week?" Roxanne's brows lifted. "Is that all it's been?" She snickered suddenly, the snuffling giggle of a little girl who knows she shouldn't be laughing. "Hey, it hasn't exactly been a week at Club Med, has it?"

"Not funny. That man scares me."

"Come on, Cat. It's over. He's history." She stood up purposefully. "You promised Charlie the bonnet chest today. Let's have a good breakfast and I'll help you finish it."

"You don't have to help. I'm only putting a second coat of varnish on it."

"The offer comes with an ulterior motive. I was hoping we could finish the chest, then shop around for a halfway decent used car."

I raised my hands. "Offer accepted. What kind of car?"

"Wheels. All I want is wheels. The cheaper, the better."

I picked up the paper and turned to the classified section, grateful for the change of topic, more than willing to accept Roxanne's certainty the nightmare was over.

I'm more timorous than I used to be. Maybe the word should be paranoid. Do fearfulness and foreboding come to the elderly because they feel themselves to be more vulnerable? Or is it because they've lived long enough to know that the human animal is the most dangerous of all the species?

I pushed it out of my head and read aloud names and prices from the used-car columns while Roxanne prepared eggs and bacon. Cassie and Brandy came in, Cassie for milk and toast, Brandy to beg for handouts.

"First we find a car, then I look for a job," Roxanne said over coffee. "I suppose summer's the wrong time to go job hunting, but I might as well make a start."

"What kind of job? What qualifications do you have?"

"Computer. Some bookkeeping. I was in stock control

at the company my grandmother worked for. I'll try them first. Maybe they'll remember me." She stood up and gathered the dishes. "Come on. Let's get that chest done."

We banished Cassie from the patio and carried the chest out. It was a perfect day for applying varnish, warm but not humid. For a while we chatted as we worked, then fell into an easy silence, rubbing the wood to a dry sheen, stopping to applaud Cassie as she flashed by on her trike circuits of the house, Brandy loping along.

As always, I was lulled by the rhythmic stroking motion required by hand-rubbed finishes, in which time loses meaning. I became aware that Roxanne had stopped working. She stood erect, buffing cloth in hand, head tilted, a frown on her face.

"Cat? Am I wrong or has it been quite a while since Cassie went by?"

Our eyes met. Simultaneously, we dropped our cloths and ran, she to the left, I to the right.

I raced up the narrow paved walkway between the side of the house and the high cedar hedge shielding me from my neighbors. No sign of Cassie. I turned the corner to the front of the house and went sprawling, hands spread, landing on my knees in the grass.

I hung there for a moment, too stunned to move, then raised my head to see what I had tripped over.

Cassie's red tricycle. Lying on its side.

I stood up painfully. Both knees were skinned raw. I bent and righted the trike and wheeled it along to the front of the house. No Cassie. No Brandy.

And no Roxanne. I felt a sharp pang of foreboding. She was a lot younger and a lot faster. I had seen her run. Her long-legged, loping grace should have carried her twice around the house by now.

I limped across the front lawn, crossed the driveway and turned the corner to the far side of the house, dragging the red trike with me.

Halfway down the stretch of lawn, Brandy lay on the grass. Roxanne knelt over her, motionless, her face hidden in a curtain of sun-streaked hair, bloodied hands raised and held out, palms up, in a pose of supplication. Brandy's white ruff and vest were stained the same scarlet.

The sunlight turned white. Every detail was imprinted with shocking clarity on my retinas.

My heart drained. I released the trike and stumbled along the path. Roxanne raised her head.

"Cat . . . Cat . . ." Her voice was a croak, her face pale with horror. She pushed her hair back from her face with shaking hands. "She's . . . they . . . Cat . . . *her throat's been cut!*"

Blood pounded in my ears. It was moments before I realized the persistent ringing accompanying it was not in my head.

The phone. The phone was ringing. I turned and ran.

In the kitchen, I snatched the phone from its cradle and screamed, "Hello?"

"I told you, don't fuck with me." There was no mistaking that reedy voice.

"What . . . where is she . . . what have you . . ." The words tumbled over one another. "For God's sake, what do you—"

"Shut up."

"I did what you wanted. Please . . . don't hurt Cassie. She's just a little girl. I did what you—"

"Shut up. Shut up or I hang up."

"Please." I drew a shuddering breath. Roxanne came through the screen door. "I'll do anything you say. Whatever you want. Just don't hurt—"

"Ten seconds. You have ten seconds to shut your fucking face." The menace projected by the thin, uninflected voice sent ice water through me. "I hang up and you'll never see the kid again. You understand? *One. Two.*"

I pressed my fingers over my mouth and waited, staring into Roxanne's eyes.

"*Three. Four. Five.*" He paused. "Now put the kid's mother on."

I held the phone out to Roxanne. She took it wordlessly.

"Yes?" she said dully. She listened, nodded, then held the phone away, staring down at it in her hand. "He hung up."

"What did he say? He said something." I took the phone from her and replaced it in its cradle. "What did he say?"

"He said . . ." She raised her hands and looked at them as though only now recognizing they were bloodstained. She turned to the sink. "He told me to be at the Lanterna Verde restaurant at four o'clock tomorrow. Then he hung up."

"The Lanterna Verde? Where's the Lanterna Verde?"

"I don't know. He didn't say." She turned on the tap, picked up the soap bar beside the sink and began washing her hands mechanically, her face frozen. "He just told me to be there and hung up."

"Did he say he'd . . ." I began. The front doorbell pealed, shattering the quiet house. Both Roxanne and I jumped as though touched by the same hot wire.

The bell rang again, then again and again, a shave-and-a-haircut beat. I ran to the front and flung the door open.

Steve was on the stoop, one foot pressing the screen door wide, one hand holding aloft a bottle of champagne.

"Break out the glasses, Cat." He swung the bottle like a bell. "We're celebrating!"

"Steve!" Steve. Grinning like a fool.

"You're not going to believe this. Some crazy producer's bought my book! Gonna make a TV movie out of it!" His grin died. "Cat? Hey. What is it? What's the matter?"

"Cassie." My throat tightened and I had to force the words out. "It's Cassie. She's been kidnapped."

"What?" He stepped into the hallway, letting the screen door slam. "Where's Roxanne?"

"In the kitchen. She's in the kitchen."

Steve thrust the bottle of wine at me and pushed past. My hands closed over the chilled, sweating glass in time to save it from crashing to the tile floor.

He crossed the kitchen in three great strides and put his arms around Roxanne. She leaned against him, trembling, and he pulled her closer.

"Just tell me where Wayne works," he growled. "I'll go after the bastard with a baseball bat."

Roxanne straightened and pulled back. "Not Wayne," she said. She turned her head away, visibly discomposed at how naturally she had accepted Steve's embrace. "It wasn't Wayne."

Steve let her go, puzzled. "What do you mean, it wasn't Wayne? Who the hell else?"

"The black car," I said. "The Jag. The men in the black Jaguar. They took Cassie. They killed Brandy."

"What? What the hell?" Steve looked from me to Roxanne. His eyes narrowed. He reached out, touched the bloodstains on her cheek, pushed back a bloody strand of hair from her face. "Where's Brandy?" he asked quietly.

"Brandy's beside the house." I gestured and realized I still held the bottle of champagne. I set it on the counter. "She's out beside the house. They . . . they c-cut her throat."

Steve looked from Roxanne to me in disbelief. He turned and slammed out the door. We heard his heavy footsteps on the patio, then nothing. We waited. Maybe it isn't true, I thought. Maybe she isn't really there.

He returned, his face set with anger.

"Get a blanket, Cat," he ordered. "An old one. I'll put her in the van. We'll take her out to my place."

I ran to the linen closet and snatched a blanket, any blanket. Steve took it from me.

"I'll come," I said.

"No." His tone brooked no argument. "Make coffee. I'll take care of Brandy. Then we'll talk."

He went outside, letting the screen door slam behind him. I stifled the impulse to run after him, like a child fearful of being left to wait alone.

"I'll make the coffee." Roxanne said the words without hearing them. She stood motionless, shoulders hunched, her eyes intent on the screen door, immobilized as I was by feelings of helplessness and dread.

"I'll make the coffee." I forced a normal tone. "You better wash your face. There's blood on it."

Roxanne turned, frowning. Her shoulders dropped and she expelled a deep breath. "Your knees!" she said, astonished. "They're all bloody."

"I fell. They're okay." I reached for the tin of coffee. Roxanne left the kitchen, returning with the first-aid kit from the bathroom.

"Sit down," she said. "I'll fix your knees."

"I'll do it. Don't fuss. Make the coffee."

She handed me the kit. We worked in depressed silence.

Steve returned, went to the sink and washed his hands. He said nothing until we sat at the table, each clutching a mug of fresh coffee.

"All right," he said. "Tell me."

I told him everything. Liverlips, the brute accompanying him, the apartment, Stella Starr, the bomb, Mrs. Karpinka. He listened without comment. Roxanne produced the morning paper. He read the paragraph about Mrs. Karpinka, then the account of the bombing, lingering over it, frowning thoughtfully.

"Organized crime," he muttered. "Organized crime. It says Starr was known to have connections with organized crime."

He stood up abruptly and went to the phone, dialing as he spoke to us over his shoulder.

"I know somebody," he said. "It might be a long shot, but maybe he—" He interrupted himself. "Mike? It's Steve. You going to be there for a while? Yeah, it's important. I'll be right over. Stay put. Wait for me."

He replaced the phone.

"I'll go get him. Don't go out, either of you. I won't be more than an hour."

He left, touching Roxanne's shoulder as he passed by her. We heard the door open, slam shut; a moment later, the sound of the van starting up, then the noise of the motor fading down the driveway. Roxanne sat motionless, her head drooping.

"Roxanne, I'm so sorry," I said miserably. "Cassie . . . it's all my fault."

"She'll be so scared. She'll be so scared." Her voice was husky with unshed tears. She raised her head. "She's never been away from me before. She won't know what's happening. She'll be so scared."

There is no anguish to match that felt by a mother whose child is in pain or danger. Knowing Roxanne's torment, I was suddenly overwhelmed with self-loathing. A stupid old woman. I felt old. Old, empty and defeated.

"If I hadn't robbed that bank—"

"You'd have lost your house."

"—you and Cassie would be safe now."

Roxanne's gaze hardened, her eyes coldly blue. "Let's not kid ourselves, okay?" she said harshly. "Cassie and I would be sitting in a women's shelter now, waiting for legal charity and handouts from Wayne. Whatever's happening, it's happening to us. You. Me. Cassie. Us." She reached across the table and placed her hand over mine. "And Brandy. Oh, Cat, I'm so sorry about Brandy."

"Brandy." I turned my head blindly, doing what I've

always done. Covering pain the way a dog buries a bone, to be dealt with later. Alone.

She released my hand, drew a shuddering breath.

"Screw it. I can't just sit on my ass and wait." She stood up abruptly. "Let's go finish the goddamn chest. You told Charlie he could pick it up today."

We went out to the patio and picked up where we'd left off. Had it been only two hours ago?

At one point I could have sworn I heard the jingling of Brandy's identity tags. I glanced over at Roxanne. She was working, solemn-faced, deep in her own thoughts. I wondered how long it would be before I stopped listening for that ghostly jingle. Sweet, silly, cowardly Brandy. How could anyone hurt such a *nebbish* dog?

I heard a car door slam. Roxanne's head reared. She slid the bonnet drawer back into the chest. I gathered the buffing rags. We looked at one another fearfully.

"Steve," I said. She nodded.

We entered the kitchen as Steve, carrying a brown file carton, appeared down the front hall. Behind him was a man, shorter and older, limping, a thick, brick-colored file docket tied with a string held against his chest.

"Cat. Roxanne." Steve set the carton on the kitchen table. "Mike Melnyk."

"Hi." The man smiled and suddenly he looked familiar. He placed his docket on the table and stretched out his hand. I took it, studying him, trying to place him.

He was shorter than Steve, under six feet, and chunky. He wore a wrinkled cotton seersucker suit over a coin-printed brown shirt, open at the collar. His hair was thin on top, almost gone. What was left was dark, with a frosting of gray. His naggingly familiar face was round and tanned, with good laugh lines around small, almost simian, sharp brown eyes. Deep grooves bracketed the smiling mouth. Late fifties. About my age. Mike Melnyk? Then I remembered.

"I thought you looked familiar! You're Michael Melnyk. The columnist? Nite Line? Page three? Picture at the top?"

He laughed, dipping his head in a gesture that was both deprecatory and gratified.

"Twenty years ago. Forty pounds ago." He passed a hand over his thinning pate. "And a fair head of hair ago. I'm surprised you remember. That was a long time ago."

"The smile hasn't changed. And you were good. I really missed your column when you quit."

"That's nice to hear." He glanced at Roxanne, his smile fading. "Roxanne? I'm sorry about Cassie. Steve told me the whole story. You've got to try to believe this. We are going to get her back."

Roxanne's face crumpled. "How?" she asked miserably.

Mike patted the files he had brought. "Hopefully, with these," he said. "And the sooner we start, the better."

"You two start," Steve said. He pulled a chair away from the table and set the carton on it. "Cat, I'm starving. Okay if Roxanne and I whip up some food?"

"For all of us." I wasn't hungry, but I desperately wanted a cup of coffee. I sat down at the table facing Mike. He untied the string on the file docket and withdrew several beige filing folders.

"We'll start with Stella Starr. The only name we have." His voice had become precise, professional. He passed a photo to me. It was a police shot of a considerably younger woman, front and side views, a number across her chest.

"Stella Staretsky, the one and only time the police were able to pin anything on her. That was fifteen years ago." He handed me another picture. "Recognize the man?" he asked.

I seized the photo. Stella and the man in the silver frame had been snapped together at an outdoor flower stand on a downtown street.

"Yes. It's the man I met in the hall as I was leaving."

Mike nodded. "Carmine Diano." He slid another photograph toward me, placed another beside it, two different pictures of the man he had identified.

"That's him." I fanned the three pictures in front of me and studied them. "Who is he? Who's Carmine Diano?"

"He calls himself a financial consultant." Mike reached into his pocket and withdrew a pack of cigarettes. He pulled out a cigarette and lit it with a plain wooden kitchen match, squinting against the sulfurous flame. "He's a corporation. Real estate. Construction. Trucking. Restaurants. A travel agency. Parking garages."

Steve left the sandwiches he was putting together, came and leaned over my shoulder to see the photos. He picked up one of them and took it to Roxanne. She looked at it and lifted her eyebrows at me. I nodded.

"That's him," I said. "He's a corporation? How does anyone get to be a corporation?"

Mike smiled. "When I first knew Carmine, he was a pimp."

I gaped at him, trying to imagine the urbane, handsome man I had seen as a procurer.

"A pimp," Mike continued. "Plus a little bit of this, a little bit of that. Truck highjacking. Mom-and-pop store heists. Shylocking. Just another small-time wiseguy."

"Couldn't have been so small-time," Steve observed. "Small-timers don't get that rich. Or do they?"

"Not hardly. Carmine got rich bankrolling drug deals. He's also in the laundry business. Washing drug money. And various other assorted enterprises." Mike squinted through the smoke from his cigarette. "Know what daisy-chaining is?" he asked.

"No." Steve shook his head.

"Corporate layering?"

"I know what corporate layering is," Steve said.

"Same idea." Mike nodded. "Drug-money launderers set up a series of interlocking legit companies and dummy corporations and move the money back and forth between them so it gets to be impossible to trace. Diano's probably got a dozen nominee owners scattered all over the world who never heard of him. I know for sure he owns a bank in Panama."

"A bank? Diano owns a bank?"

"Hey." Mike smiled humorously. "It's a room in an office building with a telephone, a Telex, a fax machine and a guy named Ramon. But it's an honest-to-God licensed bank."

"That's organized crime?" I asked. "I mean, is Diano the organized crime Stella Starr was connected with?"

"Stella was one of Diano's smurfs."

"Smurf?"

"Courier. She'd take the dirty money, bank drafts, cash and what have you, on buying trips. Wash it through one of his dummy corporations or Mickey Mouse banks." Mike butted his cigarette, lit another. "She was also Carmine's longtime doxie."

"Doxie?" I couldn't help smiling.

Mike shrugged. "Mistress. Squeeze. Moll. Whatever."

Steve brought a plateful of sandwiches, placed it on the table. He lifted the brown carton from the chair to the floor and sat down, straddling the chair.

"Tell Cat what you told me." He reached for a sandwich, bit deeply, gestured for Mike to do the same.

"In a minute." Mike waved his cigarette. He tapped the handsome face in the photograph. "Carmine was the one who was supposed to be blown away. Stella Starr was incidental."

"Incidental?" I was shocked at the word. "The woman was spattered all over her bedroom! That's incidental?"

Mike shrugged. He butted his half-smoked cigarette, took a sandwich from the plate and bit into it.

"Diano went to Starr's apartment every Tuesday and

Friday for . . . uh . . . nooners? Those two days would be about the only time he wouldn't have at least a couple of guys around."

He chewed and swallowed, gesturing with his sandwich. "If I know about the . . . uh . . . arrangement, you can be damn sure a few other people know, too. Somebody wants to off Diano, it's the perfect time, the perfect place. Starr was inci . . . what the hell, Starr went with the territory."

Roxanne set the coffeepot on the table. "If you're right— if Diano was the target, not Starr—whoever they were, they're planning to try again," she said. She went to the counter, picked up four mugs and returned to the table. "And I'm *it*."

"Makes sense." Mike nodded. "Diano's already seen Cat. So you're it. With Cassie as leverage."

"Believe me, I'll do it." Roxanne's face was stony. "I'll kill anybody they want. As many as they want. Just so I get Cassie back."

Mike hesitated, glanced at Steve. Steve took Roxanne's hand in his.

"It isn't that simple, Roxanne," he said gently. "Mike doesn't think they're going to leave anyone around who could identify them. That includes—"

"We have to put names to them," Mike interrupted sharply. He placed his hand on the docket. "There's a possibility the men we want are in here. Cat, you're the only one who's seen them. Start with the man you talked to. Describe him. Don't leave anything out, even if it seems inconsequential. Tell me everything you remember."

"Okay." I took a deep breath and let it out in an effort to release the tension I felt. "Okay. Forty to forty-five years old. About your height." I nodded at Mike. "Five ten? Five eleven? Well built. No fat. Broad shoulders. I'd guess about a hundred sixty pounds. Well dressed. Maybe a bit on the flashy . . . no, natty . . . side. Silk suit, tie. Not casual. Natty.

An expensive gold watch, Patek Philippe at least. The real thing. Big, showy gold pinky ring on his left hand. Diamonds surrounding a square-cut ruby."

"Good. Good," Mike encouraged. "Go on."

"Black hair, not too short. Styled. Blow-dried. Not just a haircut, you know?"

Mike nodded. He reached for another sandwich, his eyes never leaving my face.

"Deep tan. Dark eyes. Almost black, actually. Very scary eyes. Shiny. Glittery. No depth. No expression." I frowned. "A thin white scar on his right—no, left—cheekbone, just under the eye. Scary voice. High. Thin. Like a young boy's. No timbre." I imitated the voice as best I could. "Like this? He talks like this? Like a kid?"

Mike froze, the sandwich suspended halfway.

"Very unattractive mouth. Those dark, sort of purplish lips some people—"

"Liverlips?" Mike leaned forward.

I looked at him, startled. "Liverlips! That's what I call him in my mind. Does it ring a bell?"

Mike whistled softly through his teeth. He replaced his sandwich on the plate, reached for his docket and pulled out a new folder. He withdrew a photograph and handed it to me, his eyes narrowed, watchful.

I looked down at the photo and felt a reflexive pang of fear. Liverlips was beside the black car, either getting in or out, one leg inside. The light was good, his face clear. There was no mistaking him.

"That's him," I said, my fists clenching of their own accord. "And that's the black car. The Jaguar."

Mike pushed another glossy photo in front of me. Two men were exiting through a heavy, dark wood door to the street, unaware of the presence of a photographer.

"Liverlips." I nodded. "The other man, the big one, is the Hulk. I mean, that's what I've been calling him."

Roxanne snatched the photos. She looked from one to the other, back to the first, and raised her head, a bewildered frown on her face.

"But he's handsome!" she cried. "My God! This is a good-looking man!"

"Handsome!" My voice slid up an octave, incredulous. "Are you out of your mind? He's revolting."

Steve took the photo, studied it. "Cat." He handed the picture to me. "Take another look. Whatever else he is, the sonovabitch is a good-looking guy."

"Ugh." I shuddered. "You haven't seen him in the flesh. Maggots. Cockroaches. Everything that makes my flesh crawl." I pushed the photo at Mike. "Who is he?"

"His name is Vincenzo Pugliese." Mike edged the plate of sandwiches aside and placed yet another photograph on the table. He set it at an angle so Roxanne, Steve and I could see it—a dinner-club glossy of a group of people.

"Seated." Mike placed a finger, pointing to the nun seated at the left of the photo. "Angela, Carmine Diano's oldest daughter. Behind her, Teresa, another daughter. Next seated, Gina Diano, Carmine's wife. Carmine standing behind her. Next to Mama Diano, Vince Pugliese. Standing behind Vince, Andrea. Andrea is Vince's wife. Andrea is also Carmine's daughter."

For a moment, I didn't make the connection. Then I did.

"Liverlips is Diano's son-in-law?"

Steve picked up the photo.

"Diano's own son-in-law is trying to kill him?" he asked.

Mike nodded, preoccupied and frowning. He reached into an inside pocket of his jacket and withdrew a small black book. He licked a finger and pushed through the pages.

"Mind if I use your phone?" He was on his feet and across the kitchen while asking, dialing before I waved consent. We all waited silently.

"May I speak to Mr. Kramer," he said at last. He gazed

out the window, his face unreadable. "Thank you," he said. We waited again.

Then "Nick? It's Mike." His voice was cool, uninflected. "I've come across something you'll find interesting." He listened. "Not over the phone. Too long. Too complicated." He studied the floor, listening again. "Fine. Six-thirty is fine. I'm bringing someone with me."

He replaced the phone and stood there for a moment, head low. He rubbed his chin and turned to face us. He glanced at the wall clock behind me.

"Okay," he said. "Cat, we meet with Kramer at six-thirty. We'll have to leave in half an hour. It'll take us about half an hour to get there."

"Can I come?" Roxanne asked.

Mike shook his head. "Sorry, Roxanne."

"Who's Kramer?" Steve asked.

"Kramer." Mike's smile didn't reach his eyes. "Nick Kramer is the reason Carmine Diano will never spend a day in prison."

"How can he help?" I asked. "How can this Kramer help us?"

"I'm not sure he can," Mike admitted. "I'm not even sure he will. But right now, he's all we've got."

"Why don't we just go after this guy Vince?" Steve asked. "We know he has Cassie."

"But we don't know where," Mike replied. "And until we do, we don't go anywhere near him. Don't even think about it. The man has a built-in antenna quivering in all directions. He saw Cat at the bank for what—two seconds? In two seconds, he knows he's got something he can use. No. As long as he thinks you don't know who he is, there's a chance he won't harm Cassie."

"I can't believe he'd hurt an innocent child!" Roxanne pushed the family group photo at me. "Look at him. He looks like a normal human being! Doesn't he? Don't they all?"

135

"Do you know him?" I asked Mike.

"I've met him," Mike said.

"Who is he? What kind of man could do something like this? What kind of animal is he?"

"Vince?" Mike lit a cigarette and inhaled deeply. He blew out the match with a thin stream of smoke.

"Boys' voices change anywhere between the ages of thirteen and fifteen," he said. "Vince's didn't. At seventeen, he still had a kid's voice. What probably happened, some ignorant old country grandmother said his voice didn't change because his testicles hadn't descended. Stupid. But it got spread around. *Hey. Vincenzo Pugliese ain't got no balls.* I suppose Vince had no choice. In that neighborhood? He had to prove he had balls. Big ones."

"Balls?" I blurted angrily. "It doesn't take big balls to slit a dog's throat."

Mike turned his gaze on me and studied my face for a moment. "Cat," he said finally, "I'm sorry as hell about your dog. But it could have been Cassie. You told Diano the place was on fire. To a man as antsy as Diano, that's like a police siren. He's gone. And how much would you bet he didn't tell his son-in-law how close he came to a trip to the moon with Stella Starr?"

I stared at him, shaken, then looked at Roxanne. She was white with shock.

"Vince is a man with a very short fuse," Mike said. "And he likes to hurt people. By the time he was nineteen, nobody was messing with Vincenzo Pugliese. Carmine was shylocking in those days, and Vince went to work for him. Collecting. Which he was very good at. And being young, handsome and ambitious, he married the boss's daughter. End of story."

"Except now he wants Poppa dead," Steve said. "Why?"

"He has to be setting up a thing for himself." Mike's eyes narrowed thoughtfully. "He's been approached. That's the only way it makes sense."

"What makes sense? What do you mean?" Steve asked.

Mike looked up. "Drugs. Vince is setting up to deal."

"But why kill Diano?"

"Because Diano won't touch drugs now. He finances drug buys. He washes drug money for dealers. But he won't deal, he's way past that. Nobody in his organization is permitted to deal. If Vince starts, Diano will cut his heart out, family or not. Plus, Vince'll need money. Big money. Carmine dead, Andrea inherits."

"Why not just wait? The old man isn't going to last forever. He has no sons." Steve indicated the family photo. "Why not just sit it out until Diano dies and the whole thing drops in his lap?"

Mike shook his head. "Because that's not going to happen, even if Carmine should die tomorrow of natural causes—and Vince knows it." Mike butted his cigarette. He pushed the butt around in the ashtray. "Carmine brought in an outsider. A brain. A brain who organized Carmine with so many twists and loops nobody else has the big picture. Vince is muscle. But he's family. When Diano goes, Vince'll be a hired hand, nothing more."

"Who's the brain?" Steve was intrigued. "Do you know him?"

"Kramer. Nick Kramer."

"Kramer?" I was startled. "The man we're going to meet?"

Mike nodded.

"You have a picture of him? Of Kramer?" Steve asked.

Mike shook his head. "No pictures of Kramer." There was a flatness to the statement that discouraged further questions about Kramer.

Roxanne had been listening silently, her eyes cast down, studying one photo, then another, over and over.

"How do you know so much about all these people?"

"Mike's writing a book," Steve said.

"About these people?"

"Them. People like them," Mike said. He glanced at the clock. "Cat? You should get changed. Place we're going isn't the Ritz, but it isn't a greasy spoon either."

"Where are we going?"

"The Capri. A restaurant."

"Give me two minutes."

In the bedroom, I stepped out of soiled shirt and shorts, reached for the pink suit and reflected I'd dressed up more often in the past three weeks than I had in the past three years. From the kitchen, without being able to make out the words, I could hear the rumble of Steve's voice, the quieter pitch of Mike's responses.

I dabbed on lipstick, slipped into the Amalfis, snatched up a handbag and returned to the kitchen. Mike's brows lifted in approval and he nodded.

"Two minutes on the nose." He stood up. "Let's go."

I walked around the table, bent over Roxanne and hugged her shoulders. She leaned against me for a heartbeat.

"We'll be back as soon as possible," I said and added with as much confidence as I could muster, "Roxanne. It's going to be all right."

She nodded, her smile strained. "I know, Cat."

Reaching for my car keys, I remembered Charlie.

"Steve? Charlie and Rafe are coming to pick up the bonnet chest. Tell them there are only two coats of varnish on it. If they want three, tell them they'll have to wait."

"Cat," Steve said dryly, "stop dithering. Go already."

I snatched the keys off the hook and left the kitchen, Mike following. We stepped out of the house into the hot glare of the late afternoon sun.

"You want to drive?" I offered him the keys.

He shook his head. "I'm a lousy driver. You drive."

He limped around the car, opened the door and slid into the passenger seat. He sat slumped, a preoccupied frown on his face. He was silent, deep in thought, as I turned out of the driveway and onto the street. At the cross street, I waited for him to come to the surface.

"Mike," I said finally, "I hate to interrupt. But you're going to have to tell me where we're going."

"Sorry." He roused himself. "All the way downtown. It's on Jefferson. Near Riverview. Know where that is?"

I nodded, lifted my foot from the brake and the car sped forward. Mike lit a cigarette. I inhaled the pungent tobacco odor with sudden longing.

"Can I have one of those?"

"A cigarette? Sure." He handed me the lit cigarette, dug out another. "I didn't think you smoked."

"I quit two years ago. For the fifth time."

I inhaled deeply, felt the smoke hit the back of my throat and sighed, knowing I was going to have to quit for a sixth time. We drove in silence for a block and stopped for a red light. I side-glanced at him and caught him studying me, his brows drawn together.

"What?" I asked.

"You interest me strangely." He tilted his head, squinting through a smoke ring.

I laughed out loud. "My God. It has to be thirty years since anybody used that phrase."

He grinned. A clown's grin. "I got a lot of mileage out of that in my salad days." The grin widened. "My motives were a little bit different then."

"I'll bet they were. What's motivating you now?"

"Curiosity."

The light changed. I turned my attention to the road.

"You described Vince," he continued. "Very specific. All the details. Not many people see that much. So I'm curious."

"No big deal." I rolled down the side window and threw the cigarette out. "I used to be a TV producer. Commercials, not shows. You're involved with locations, settings, casting, wardrobe, props. Details are important, even minor details. They add up to create the image you're trying for. I suppose I tend to be aware of details."

"Television commercials." He sounded amused. "Plan a bank robbery the way you plan a television commercial?"

I glanced at him. "As a matter of fact, I did."

"Did your scenario include blowing it?"

I had to change lanes in rush-hour traffic and nobody was giving an inch. I concentrated on driving and didn't answer until a white-haired woman in a beatup green van gestured me in ahead of her. I waved my thanks.

"I was mad," I told Mike. "Mad as in angry. Probably mad as in crazy, too. I don't remember even considering that it might not work. I wasn't thinking too clearly at the time."

"Wasn't there some other way? Couldn't you have borrowed the money?"

I turned my head to look at him. "Would you lend me thirty-five thousand dollars?" I asked.

"Could you pay it back?"

"Sure. About a thousand a year."

"How old are you?"

"Sixty."

"Ninety five?" He chuckled. "Hell, I don't expect to live that long."

"Neither do I."

The Jefferson Street off-ramp loomed ahead. I slowed into the exit feeder lane behind a trailer truck and took the long, slow curve down to Jefferson into a logjam of cars, backed up by a traffic light a block away. Mike was quiet as we waited for an opening.

"Is this man Kramer a friend of yours?" I asked.

"Uh," he grunted noncommittally.

The line of cars began moving. I insinuated myself into a three-foot gap, intimidating a young woman in a new red sport car. Not a scratch on the shiny surface. She stabbed at me with an upraised middle finger, mouthing her air-conditioned epithets. We crawled to the traffic light.

"Can he do anything? Will he help?"

Mike shrugged without answering.

The light clicked from red to green. I drove through the intersection and continued down Jefferson. I glanced across at him, wanting reassurance from him. He was slumped, staring moodily at the smoke curling from his cigarette, wrapped in his own space, shutting me out as effectively as if he had closed a door.

Jefferson began changing from commercial to residential, with here and there a cluster of small shops. A florist's, a convenience store, a hairdresser's. No cafes, no snack bars, no restaurants. We were approaching Riverview. After Riverview, nothing but water shimmering and flashing diamonds under the slanting rays of the westering sun.

"Mike?"

Mike straightened. He flipped his cigarette butt through the open window and leaned forward, gesturing ahead to my left.

"Slow down. The big house with the white pillars. That's the Capri."

27

$\mathcal{U}$nless you were familiar with the Capri, you could pass it a dozen times without being aware it was there. Other than the name Capri in gold script on the fanlight above the oak doors, there was no sign identifying the old red brick mansion as a restaurant.

A circular driveway passed under a white-pillared *porte cochere* before arcing back into the street. Dense cedar hedges flanking the drive's entry and exit hid the major portion of the house and surroundings from view to passing traffic. Centered in the barbered lawn of the half moon created by the driveway was a bed of flaming calla lilies.

I waited for a couple of cars to pass, then made a left turn into the drive. Behind the screen of hedge on the right, a road ran alongside the house.

"Park in front," Mike ordered. "Under the porch."

"It says *Parking in Rear*." I pointed to the discreet arrow planted in the grass.

"That's for paying customers. We're not going to be here that long."

Somewhat dubiously, I parked where instructed and climbed out of the car. Mounting the three slate steps leading to the oak door, Mike's limp was more pronounced. He took the stairs one at a time, first stepping up with his right leg and then hitching his left leg up to the new level. The truculent expression on his face stifled any impulse I had to offer help.

We stepped through the oak doors into the twilight coolness of air conditioning that smelled faintly of the sea.

We were in a large central hall paneled in dark wood. Facing us, a broad staircase rose several steps to a landing, then turned on itself to rise to the floor above. A tall, stained-glass window in a rainbow of colors filtered sunlight down onto the rich cobalt-blue rug under our feet.

Centered on the triangular wall created by the staircase was a fountain, incongruous in that setting. It was a gilt lighthouse, five feet tall, mounted on pearlescent rocks in a pool the shape of a massive clamshell. Luminous sea gulls mounted on fine, silvery wire dipped and swayed in the current of scented air.

To our right, a room that had, in all likelihood, been the mansion's parlor was now a barroom. Circular pedestal tables surrounded by comfortable black-leather armchairs filled three-quarters of the room. The bar was of padded black leather, backed by smoky mirrors and fronted with high-backed leather bar stools. Hanging crystal goblets gleamed in the discreet spotlights aimed from the ceiling above the bar. A pyramid of black glass shelves displayed bottles of liquor in every size and shape booze comes in.

At the far end of the bar, a man half stood, half sat on one of the stools, a telephone held to his ear. A blue-coated waiter, seeing us, left the table he was setting. He spoke to the man at the bar, gestured in our direction.

"That's Kramer," Mike said quietly. "The man at the bar."

Kramer nodded to the waiter. He set the phone down on the bar and came to meet us.

Combine three parts of Robert Taylor's flawless good looks with one part of the faintly sinister sleekness of George Raft—if you're old enough to know what I'm talking about. Throw them into a blender and you'll have the glimmering of Nick Kramer. He was the most stunningly handsome man I'd ever seen, on-screen or off.

He wasn't tall, five-eleven at most, and he walked with the feline grace of the natural athlete. He wore a sage-green cotton shirt tucked into white jeans. White boat shoes. His hair was black, flowing back from a widow's peak, the sides brushed back above small, well-shaped ears. His facial features were impossibly perfect: slim, classic nose; large, sea-green eyes half hidden by thick black lashes under arched brows. I was staring almost open-mouthed as he approached.

"Hello, Mike," he said. His head dipped in the barest nod of greeting.

"Nick." Mike's mouth curved, not quite a smile. "I'd like you to meet Cat. Catherine Wilde. Nick Kramer."

Kramer nodded briefly in my direction and gestured to the waiter hovering at the bar entrance.

"Mario, please seat Mr. Melnyk in the dining room." He turned his gaze back on Mike. "I have someone waiting on the phone. Order whatever you like. I won't be long."

We trailed Mario's splay-footed duck walk to the dining room, on our left. Everything about Mario was pear-shaped. The bald area at the rear of his skull, his head flowing into a fleshy neck, narrow shoulders above massive buttocks.

He pulled a chair back from a table midway in the room.

"Madam?" he smiled.

"Thank you." I bent and he slid the chair expertly under me, an action most waiters perform awkwardly.

He directed his smile at Mike. "Is this table suitable?"

"Fine. Great." Mike seated himself, hitched his chair up to the table. "This is fine."

"May I bring you something from the bar? Madam?"

I glanced at Mike. He shrugged.

"Please," I said. "A bloody Caesar."

Mario dipped his head, smile intact. "And for you, sir?"

"The same," Mike said indifferently. His attention was focused on the entrance to the dining room, through which we could see across the foyer into the bar.

"Very good, sir." Mario leaned past me, flicked a switch on the lamp centerpiece, a miniature of the lighthouse in the foyer, and waddled away.

Not exactly a greasy spoon, Mike had said. And it wasn't.

The room had been decorated, I assumed, to represent a patio on the Isle of Capri, overlooking the Mediterranean. The walls were mistily romantic seacoast frescoes, reasonably well painted. Banquettes upholstered in the deep blue of the rug lined three walls. Ten large circular tables occupied the center of the room. Below the sky-blue ceiling, a latticework of pale wood supported a variety of hanging plants, some in lavish bloom. They could have been plastic or silk. Or they may have been real. Whichever, they created an effect of dining in a bower.

"Quite a place," I said.

Mike turned back to me. He delved in his pocket and tossed out his pack of cigarettes, then began scrabbling for a light.

"Left my bloody matches on your kitchen table."

"Here." Boat shoes and thick pile had prevented us from hearing Nick Kramer's approach. He tossed a blue folder of matches on the table, pulled back the chair opposite Mike and dropped into it. "Still won't use a lighter?"

"Keep losing the damn things." Mike shook a cigarette from the crumpled pack.

"Can I bum one?" I asked. There was a perceptible tension between the two men that put me on edge.

"Sure." Mike handed me the cigarette and struck a match.

I leaned forward, sucked in the smoke gratefully as Mario arrived with a tray. He placed our drinks in front of us and poured Perrier over ice in a glass for Kramer. Kramer pointed at the cigarette pack and held up two fingers. Mario nodded.

"How've you been?" Kramer studied Mike through half-lidded eyes, thick black lashes shadowing the green of the iris.

"Fine. Just fine." Mike lit his cigarette, squinting past the flare of the match.

"How's the leg?"

"Like always. Pain in the butt."

Mario returned. He dropped two packs of cigarettes on the table. Kramer nodded his thanks, turned his head a bare inch to watch Mario's receding back.

"How's the book going?" he asked.

"It marches," Mike replied tersely.

Their gazes locked. Seconds ticked by silently, twenty of them. There was a conversation going on I couldn't hear.

Kramer ended it.

"So," he said. "What is it I'd find interesting? That's what you said? Interesting?"

"I think I said *very interesting*. Tell him, Cat."

With no change of expression, a minimum movement of his head, Kramer transferred his attention to me.

"Oh." I was disconcerted. I had assumed Mike would carry the ball. I hadn't prepared myself and had no idea of where to start. "Well," I fumbled. "I was robbing a bank . . ."

I stopped.

The green eyes had snapped wide, an angry glint in their depths. Kramer swung on Mike.

Mike raised his hands, palms forward. "No joke." The laugh lines around his eyes creased with amusement. "Don't let the garden-club getup fool you. This lady packs a mean plastic knife. Cat? Maybe you better take it from the top."

Those eyes, half-lidded once more, fixed on me in a flat, appraising stare. "Names. Places. Dates." Kramer shifted in his chair, one elbow on the arm of his chair, the other on the table, hand placed palm down. "From the beginning."

Starting from Daisy's phone call, I gave him the who, what, why, where, when and how. Mort. Simpson-Simpkins, whichever. Saul Vineberg. The trashing of my house and the realization that I would lose it. The bank robbery. Roxanne and Cassie. The black car. Wayne. Dorothy Atkins. Steve. Our retrieval of Roxanne's possessions. I refused to refer to it as burglary. The black car.

Other than the merest twitch at the corner of his mouth when I described the bank action, Kramer listened without movement, never taking his eyes from my face. I'm positive he didn't blink once. His absolute stillness first made me uneasy, then produced a peculiar reaction. The undivided attention and the direct gaze from those truly amazing eyes were hypnotic. I'd have told the man anything he wanted to know.

He stiffened almost imperceptibly when I related the first confrontation with Liverlips and the Hulk. The extravagant black lashes drooped lower when I told him of my part in the murder of Stella Starr.

"They took Cassie this morning." I couldn't control the tremor in my voice. "And they killed my dog."

Unexpected tears blurred my sight for a moment. I blinked them back and reached for a cigarette. Kramer flicked a slim gold lighter. He held the flame for me, his gaze on Mike.

"You're sure it was Vince." Kramer's tone made a statement of the question. "No mistake."

"No way," Mike said. "She identified him from photos. Him and Luigi both."

"Luigi?" I blew out a lungful of smoke. "Who's Luigi?"

"Luigi Caruso. Guy you called the Hulk," Mike explained. "His name's Luigi Caruso."

Kramer turned the lighter in his hand thoughtfully, once, twice. He looked up, from me to Mike and back.

"Mrs. Wilde. Catherine, if I may." I nodded. "Before we discuss how I might be able to help, I wonder if you'd mind coming upstairs with me. There's someone I'd like you to talk to. You too, Mike. Would you mind?"

Mike shrugged and we pushed away from the table.

Ascending the oak staircase was a slow process, Mike pulling himself up by the banister, one stair at a time. Kramer matched his pace to Mike's, his hands tucked into the rear pockets of his jeans, the span of his elbows forcing me to follow two stairs behind.

When they reached the landing and turned to mount the second flight, Mike's face was flushed and belligerent. I felt a rush of commiseration that turned to a quick flare of anger when I glanced at Kramer. He was smiling broadly, his eyes glinting with amusement at Mike's discomfort.

At the top of the stairs, Kramer gestured us to the hallway on our left. We passed four doors opening on private dining rooms furnished with circular tables large enough to seat at least eight diners. High-backed oak chairs were placed against the walls.

The hall ended in a pair of heavy oak doors. Kramer rapped twice on the right-hand door, opened it and ushered us into a room that would have set Charlie and Rafe sobbing with lust.

Paintings were massed on one wall. I recognized an oil by Mary Cassatt, a Toulouse-Lautrec drawing. Directly across, above an exquisite Regency mahogany and ormulu library table, displayed on illuminated glass shelving, was a magnificent collection of jade carvings in colors ranging from lavender to a lustrous deep green.

Seated in front of an antique eight-leaf coromandel screen, behind a marquetry and rosewood desk, was Carmine Diano. The setting diminished him. Poised against the ageless purity of that splendorous screen, he was a false note, a tinny reproduction.

He rose and circled the desk, smiling.

"There she is." He took my hand in both of his. "The beautiful bank robber who saved my life."

"How . . ." Mike began, frowning.

"This is Mrs. Wilde," Kramer interrupted. There was a steely edge to his voice. "I wanted you to hear it directly from her. Vince set up the bomb."

Diano hesitated. He dropped my hand. "She's sure?"

"She identified him from Mike's files."

"I see." Diano's eyes flicked to Mike. "Hello, Mike," he said, his smile restored.

Mike was frowning. "Carmine," he acknowledged curtly.

"I'll fill you in on the details later," Kramer said. "Right now we have a more urgent problem. Vince kidnapped a little girl, the daughter of a friend of Mrs. Wilde."

Diano looked from me to Kramer, back at me. "Why? What would that get him?"

"He ordered Roxanne to be at a restaurant tomorrow," I explained. "The Lanterna Verde? He said he'd kill Cassie if Roxanne wasn't there at four o'clock tomorrow."

Both Diano and Kramer turned on me, startled.

"You didn't tell me that," Kramer said sharply. "You're sure he said the Lanterna Verde? Tomorrow?"

"Yes. I'm sure."

Diano's eyes narrowed at Kramer. "What do you think?"

Kramer shrugged. "His grandmother was a Borgia."

For a fleeting second, the expression on Diano's face was murderous. Then it was gone. He turned on a smile for me.

"Please." He gestured to a pair of Georgian library chairs upholstered in a rich blue tapestry. "Won't you sit down? I can see we have matters to discuss."

He circled the desk, talking as he seated himself. He placed his elbows on the patined wood and clasped his hands under his chin.

"I owe you an apology, Mrs. Wilde. I'm afraid I told my son-in-law about your warning. My fault. I tend to trust people I consider close to me. However. What's done is done. I, personally, do not hold you responsible in any way. You did what you had to do. Nobody can fault you for that. But we will take it from here. We will deal with it."

Suddenly that honey-coated voice grated on me. Diano had used a lot of words to say nothing. I wondered if he'd even heard Kramer tell him of Cassie's abduction. I directed my question at Kramer.

"Will he return Cassie if Roxanne does whatever it is he wants her to do?"

"No," Kramer stated flatly.

The unequivocal word stabbed me. I looked across at Mike. He had been slumped in his chair, scowling at the floor. He turned the scowl on Kramer.

"What's this Lanterna Verde business all about?"

Kramer was slouched against the library table, his arms crossed over his chest, his legs crossed at the ankles. He lifted his gaze from his boat shoes to Mike.

"Tomorrow is Carmine's sixty-fifth birthday. Vince runs the Lanterna Verde. Tomorrow over two hundred guests will be there at a birthday dinner for Carmine. Vince will have hired extra help."

Mike's face sharpened. "Borgia. Roxanne poisons Carmine."

Kramer shrugged.

I reached in my purse for the pack of cigarettes Kramer had supplied. "Roxanne poisons Carmine?" I echoed. "Believe me, she'll do it. To save Cassie? She'll poison the whole damn lot of you." I withdrew a cigarette from the pack and held it. I had nothing to light it with. "So now that Carmine isn't going to die tomorrow, what happens to Cassie?"

Kramer didn't reply. He came to me, his lighter ready. He flicked it and held the flame for me. Looking up into that expressionless face, I had a sudden chilling thought.

"Or maybe she's already dead."

Kramer shook his head. "No. She's alive. Vince will call you. He'll make her talk or cry so you'll know she's all right. Possibly tonight. Certainly tomorrow. She's alive."

Mike pushed himself up from his chair. He placed his hands flat on the desk and leaned into Diano's face.

"She's alive," he said in a softly menacing voice. "And she'll stay alive till Roxanne walks into the Lanterna Verde. Unless you do something stupid. Unless you blow the wind up Vince's ass. Then she's dead. *Don't do it.*"

He turned his back on Diano and spoke directly to Kramer.

"We're here because I'm hoping you might know where he'd have her stashed. After we get her back, you can feed Vince Pugliese to the fishes. Until then, I'm asking you to find out where she is. And I want a promise from you— from you for him—" Mike thumbed over his shoulder at Diano, "that nobody will lay a finger on Vince until she's safe."

"You've got it," Kramer said.

Suddenly, quietly, a thickset man with the heavy, sorrowing eyes of an El Greco saint appeared in the doorway. He glanced curiously at me, then focused on Diano.

"Your guests have arrived, Mr. Diano," he said.

"Thank you, Gino." Diano rose from behind the desk. "Tell them I'll be right down."

Gino nodded and was gone.

I stood up as Diano circled the desk. He placed his hands on my shoulders and tilted his head at me.

"I hope you will consider me a friend, Mrs. Wilde." The oleaginous voice flowed over me. "A friend who owes you a debt he can never repay."

To my astonishment and dismay, he bent and pressed his lips to my cheek. *To barf,* Laurie's term of utter distaste, flashed through my mind. He must have felt my reaction. He let his hands drop and turned to Mike.

"We've had our differences, Mike," he said. "But I want

you to know how grateful I am to you for alerting me. I owe you. I owe you my life."

"Save it, Carmine." Mike's voice was heavy with dislike. "I wouldn't piss down your throat if your guts were on fire."

Diano shook his head sorrowfully. "Mike, Mike," he said, "you've become a bitter old man."

Mike grinned his clown's grin. "Not bitter, Carmine. Nasty. I've become a nasty old man."

Diano spread his hands in a gesture of helpless regret. He turned away from us and left the room.

For a moment, none of us moved. It was as though we were waiting for the air in the room to renew and freshen itself. Then Kramer pushed away from the library table, crossed to the desk and tore a page from a scratch pad. He reached in a drawer for a pen.

"Give me a number where I can reach you," he said to Mike. "Somewhere I can call all night if I have to."

Mike looked at me. I gave Kramer my phone number. He wrote it down and pushed the scrap of paper into his shirt pocket.

"It could be late when I call," he warned. "And you may have to move fast."

"We'll be ready," Mike said.

"Good." Kramer glanced from Mike to me. "Well. That's it, I guess. I'll see you to your car."

Descending the stairs was easier for Mike. He dropped from one step to the next. Kramer matched his speed. I followed behind. We could hear the murmuring of voices, spates of laughter, the muted strains of background music. Waiters were hustling in the bar. In the dining room, more than half the tables were occupied.

I thought I caught a flick of amusement on Kramer's face when he saw where the car was parked. As I turned the key in the ignition, he leaned in through the window to speak to Mike.

"I'll do everything I can, Mike," he promised.

"I know." Mike nodded, then added so quietly I was barely able to hear the words, "Take care of yourself, Nicholai."

"I will, Pop," Kramer answered softly.

He stepped back from the car. Mike gestured ahead.

"Let's go, Cat."

As I took the curve away from the portico, he leaned out the window and called back to Kramer.

"Hey, Nick. Tell Carmine his *Godfather* act sucks."

I glanced in the rearview mirror. Kramer was standing on the slate steps, watching us leave. He was laughing.

28

"He called you Pop."

I had driven four blocks with Mike slumped and silent in the passenger seat beside me.

"Eh?" Mike stirred. "What did you say?"

"I said he called you Pop."

Mike grunted. He tamped a cigarette on the back of his hand, searched his pockets and finally pressed the lighter on the dashboard. When it sprang back, he lit his cigarette, blew a cloud of smoke and turned in the seat to face me, his back to the door.

"What did you think of him?" he asked.

"Kramer?" I glanced at Mike. He was watching me narrowly. "That has to be the most beautiful man I've ever seen."

Mike snorted in disgust. "Come on, Cat."

"Okay, okay. Give me a minute."

I recalled Nick to the screen in my mind. His eyes, green flint unreadable behind the smudge of thick black lashes. The impassive face. His stillness. No projection at all. But an absence of body language is in itself body language.

"Control." I pulled to a stop as the traffic light clicked from orange to red. "Very controlled. He struck me as a man who knows exactly what he's doing. Always." Then I remembered Kramer on the staircase landing. "I didn't like him."

"You didn't?" Mike sounded surprised. "Why not?"

"Why not? The only time I saw him smile was when you were going up the stairs." The light changed to green. I pressed down on the accelerator. "I don't particularly like people who think a disability is funny."

There was no reaction from Mike. I glanced at him again. He was gazing bemusedly at the floor, a broad smile on his face.

"What's so funny?"

He raised his head as I turned my attention back to the road. I could sense his eyes on me. Then, as though he had come to a decision, he shifted his position.

"There's a tavern about a block and a half up the road. Nice neighborhood-type pub. The Griffon. Pull in there. I'll buy you a beer."

29

"Twenty years ago. July sixth." Mike set down his glass. He wiped foam from his upper lip with the back of his hand. "It was Meg's fortieth birthday. My wife. We went out for dinner. Meg, me. Meg's sister Mary and Mary's husband Stan. Stan Thomas, the sportswriter. Remember him?"

"No. But I was never much of a sports fan."

"He was a first-rate sportswriter. Right up there with the best." Mike's mouth twisted sourly. "Outside of that, he was an obnoxious asshole and a compulsive gambler who thought he could get away with anything because he was Stan Thomas. But what the hell. Mary loved him. Meg loved Mary. And I loved Meg. So . . ."

Mike drained his beer. He raised his brows. "You ready for another?"

I held up my glass, still two-thirds full. Mike waved to the waiter, pointed at his empty glass.

"We came out of the restaurant about nine-thirty. Stan's car was parked at the curb a couple of storefronts down. A brand-new, canary-yellow T-bird. Which tells you a lot about how stupid Stan had to be. Cruising in that flashy boat was like giving the finger to every bookie and loan shark he owed money to. That stupid bastard owed everybody in town."

With a cigarette hanging between his lips, Mike began his search for a light. The waiter appeared beside him, whisked away his empty glass, replaced it with a full one and dropped a packet of matches on the table. Mike handed him some bills and waved away the change. The waiter vanished.

"This is the way it happened." Mike scratched a match and lit his cigarette. "Meg and Mary were in the back seat. Stan was behind the wheel and I got into the front passenger seat. It was a hot night. I told Stan to hold it, I wanted to take off my jacket. I got out of the car. I had one arm out of my jacket when Stan turned the key in the ignition. The whole bloody world exploded. Somebody slammed me in the chest with a sledgehammer and somebody else picked me up and threw me against a brick wall."

Mike paused. He raised his glass to his lips, then set it down without drinking.

"I blacked out for a couple of minutes. Then I was being dragged across the pavement. Someone was scrabbling through my jacket, pulling at my tie. I passed out and woke up two days later in a hospital bed. My sister Maddy was there, and she's the one who had to tell me the others were dead."

He raised his glass and drank down half the beer. I groped for a cigarette from the pack on the table.

"Then," Mike set his glass down, "poor old Maddy, she had to tell me my left leg had been amputated above the knee."

"Oh." I looked at Mike helplessly. He had reported the events so factually, I had no words.

"Hey. It was a long time ago," Mike said gently. He pulled a match from the packet, struck it and held it for me. "The pain's long gone. It's like the ache I sometimes feel in the foot that isn't there any longer. The memory of pain. We've all got some of that, so let's not waste time on it."

He smiled and circled his glass with both hands.

"To understand the rest of this, you have to know what

my sister Maddy was like," he said. "Ninety percent of it was her doing."

Mike pushed his glass away, butted his cigarette and lit a fresh one. He began talking. . . .

30

... *M*y mother died when I was four. Maddy was sixteen. Years later, when I thought of my parents, the only face I'd see was my sister Maddy's. My father worked in a steel mill. When he wasn't working, he was out drinking or he was asleep. Maddy always claimed he wasn't like that before Ma died. Maybe so. All I knew of him was his silence. I don't think the man said more than ten words a year. There was a song that came out when I was in my teens—

> One night I saw upon the stair,
> A little man who wasn't there.
> He wasn't there again today.
> Oh, how I wish he'd go away.

I figured that was my pop. He just wasn't there. Maddy ran the house. Ran me. She's the one brung me up.

She was teaching by the time I hit high school. Then the old man developed cancer and she quit so she could take care of him. After he died, she married Peter Svarich. A teacher. A helluva nice guy. They were two sides of the same coin, Maddy and Pete.

I lived with them until the baby came, a boy they named Michael after me. Then I went off to college. Not because I was all that high on going, because I wasn't. I went to get Maddy and Pete off my back. To them, education was right up there with sainthood.

The Christmas Mikey was three, a drunk driver went

through a red light and broadsided Pete's van. That sonovabitch was pissed out of his mind and he walked away without a scratch. The van was totaled. Mikey was killed and
Pete ended up in a wheelchair, paralyzed from the waist
down.

Maddy was luckier. She only had cuts and bruises and a
broken leg. I dropped out of school. It was my turn to take
care of Maddy. She was a basket case.

It was Pete who nagged her into going back to school.
Not to teach. She'd always been terrific with children, and
he pushed her into qualifying to teach the handicapped.
We sold the house, rented a place closer to the college, and
the following fall we trotted back to school, Maddy and I.
Pete set himself up as a tutor and research assistant, both
of which he was very good at. He ended up with more work
than he could handle. We tried to make him cut back, he'd
never been a particularly robust man. But he said he was
having too much fun. Damn, I respected that man.

Maddy graduated at the head of her class. She was offered a good job in Texas at a school for handicapped kids
and they decided to take it. The winters here were too hard
on Pete.

They'd been there ten years when Pete died. By then,
Maddy was running the school and she decided to stay. She
liked Texas. She was proud as hell of her school and the
work they were doing. And she loved those kids.

When I opened my eyes in the hospital that day and saw
her face I cried like a baby. Shit. I was forty years old. I'd
been a police reporter and a columnist for fifteen years. I
thought I was tough. But when I saw Maddy's face, I broke
down and cried like a goddamn baby.

It's funny. As a young woman, Maddy was plain. At
fifty-two, she was beautiful. Her hair was white. Her eyes
were a bright, clear blue. And intelligent. What's the word
I'm looking for? Compassionate. She had compassionate
eyes. And the sweetest smile this side of the angels.

After the first couple of days, the police and reporters were gone. A few friends dropped by. They didn't stay long. Hell, I don't blame them. I was mean as a snake. A total pain in the ass. Even the nurses were pissed off. Maddy put up with me, God knows how. She came early and she stayed late. I'd wake up and she'd be there. She'd look up from her book and smile as if she'd forgotten how unpleasant I'd been a couple of hours before.

One afternoon, the third week I was there, I was half drowsing, half asleep, half floating on pain killers, when I heard my name way out there somewhere.

". . . Michael Melnyk?"

"Yes. It is." I could hear the smile in Maddy's voice.

"Is he asleep? He's not in a coma or something?"

I opened my eyes and there's this kid standing at the foot of the bed, staring at me with the greenest eyes I've ever seen. Black hair slicked back with a wet comb. Faded khaki T-shirt and cut-off ragged jeans. He had a paper bag clutched in a grubby hand. I figured him to be ten, maybe twelve years old. A kid.

"Who the hell are you?" I snarled at him.

"Mike," Maddy protested.

"It's okay." The kid looked at her, then turned those eyes back on me. "Nick. I'm Nick Kramer."

"Okay. You're Nick Kramer. So, Nick Kramer, why don't you turn around and march your skinny ass out of here?"

"Mike! For heaven's sake." Maddy snapped her book closed. She smiled at the kid. "I'm not bragging about it, but I'm his sister. My name's Maddy. Why don't you tell me why you've come to see Mike?"

The kid's glance bounced back and forth between Maddy and me. "They said on TV that he owes his life to whoever put the tourniquet on his leg. That whoever it was tied it on saved his life. That was me. I tied his tie on his leg."

"Like hell you did." I ignored Maddy's frown.

The kid walked around the bed. He reached into his paper bag, brought out my wallet and handed it to me.

"Yeah. So?" I hadn't known it was missing. "So you found my wallet."

"I didn't find it. I stole it."

Maddy cut me off with a venomous look. "Nick, why don't you tell us about it?" she urged.

"The car blew up." Nick spoke across the bed. "I dragged him away when it started to burn. He was out cold, but he sort of came to when I was going through his jacket looking for his wallet. So I pretended I was going for his tie and I took it off him. His leg was all bashed up and bleeding real bad, so I wrapped the tie above his knee and tightened it with a stick, like I read somewhere. Then I took his wallet and beat it."

I opened my wallet. The credit cards were there.

"Where'd my forty bucks go?"

"I borrowed it."

"You mean you stole it." I snapped the wallet closed and slid it under the pillow. "So I owe you my life. You want it? Take it."

The boy's unnatural composure crumpled. He was a kid. A momentarily very confused kid.

"I . . . your life? I . . . I don't want your life."

"You want a reward? You got it. Forty bucks. That's about what my life's worth. Keep the forty bucks."

"Mike. For heaven's sake. Give the boy a chance." Maddy smiled across the bed at the kid. "Go on, Nick."

"I want him to take my sister."

I laughed. "Your sister?" I leered at Maddy. "Give him a chance, eh? You know what we've got here? A fucking Tijuana pimp. Hey, meestair, you wanna fuck my seestair?"

The kid's face turned white, his eyes a murderous green glass.

"Shut up, Mike. Just shut up," Maddy snapped.

I shut up. Not because of Maddy. I was coping with the stab of fear that green glare had generated. Frightened by a twelve-year-old?

Maddy rose from her chair and leaned across the bed, her blue eyes intent on the boy's face.

"Nick? Where is your sister?" she asked.

He thumbed at the open door. "She's out there."

"Go get her." Maddy waited until the boy had gone, then turned angrily on me. "*You.* You miserable— You behave yourself."

Nick returned, leading a little girl by the hand. She hung back, hiding behind his shoulder, pressing herself to his back. He brought her to the foot of the bed.

"It's okay," he whispered to her. He freed his hand from hers and placed his arm around her shoulders. He directed his words at Maddy. "This is my sister Tasha," he said.

She was maybe eight years old, same green eyes, same black hair. I've seen expensive Italian dolls like her. Chinese dolls? Transparent, porcelain skin. Ivory skin. And fragile. The ethereal waif look that saints and angels have in Renaissance paintings. I've forgotten what she was wearing. I don't think I noticed.

"Hello, Tasha," Maddy said softly. "I'm Maddy. This is my brother Mike."

Tasha turned her face away, pressed into her brother.

"She doesn't talk very much." Nick's arm tightened around his sister. "She's shy."

"I know," Maddy said. "Strange faces. Strange places. They can be scary. I was that way. Everywhere but at home." Maddy smiled at Nick. "Where do you live, Nick?"

Nick's face closed down. He and Maddy could have been the only ones in the room, green eyes locked with blue. Seconds ticked by.

"Nicky." Maddy broke the silence, her voice gentle. "When you leave the hospital, where will you go?"

163

"I don't know."

Maddy nodded as though he had answered correctly. "Well," she said, "would you like to have dinner with me tonight? I'm all alone in Mike's big house. I'd like the company if you'd like to come."

"Okay," the kid said stiffly. Then the green eyes thawed a degree. "I mean, yes. Thank you."

"Good." Maddy glanced at her watch. "If we leave now, we can pick up a pizza and be home by six. Or would you rather have fried chicken?"

The kid shrugged and Maddy turned to me.

"You don't mind if I leave now?"

"Would it matter if I did?"

She bent and kissed my cheek. "I'll call you," she said.

"Don't bother."

She left with the two kids. I spent the evening snarling at the nurses.

In the morning, she phoned to tell me she wouldn't be in until late in the day. I told her as far as I was concerned she didn't have to come at all. She hung up on me.

Two days later, when they wheeled me back to my room after X rays, she was in her usual chair, a book in her lap, a smile on her face.

"Hi, Grumpy," she said.

"Huh." I was so damn glad to see her and at the same time, sour and angry with her for having deserted me. "So what did you do with Huck Finn?"

"They're at home. Nick's cutting the grass and Tasha's weeding Meg's vegetable garden."

I reared up, dumbfounded. "You left that thief alone in my house? For Christ's sake, Maddy, have you gone senile? That little bastard'll go through the house like shit through a goose. Jesus Christ, he's probably got a truck backed up to the front door right now."

"Sure he has. He's got a truck. And a warehouse to stash

the stuff. And a fence to peddle it," Maddy said tartly. "For heaven's sake, Mike. He's twelve years old."

"Like hell. That kid's no twelve-year-old. He's a midget. A forty-year-old midget gangster."

Maddy burst out laughing. God, Maddy had a magnificent laugh. For a woman who'd had little enough to laugh over in her life, she had the greatest laugh I've ever heard, then or since. I was furious, after a while less so, and finally I couldn't help snorting. Grudgingly.

Her laughter subsided. "Mikey. We have to talk."

"Talk? About what?"

"About you. But first I'm going to tell you about those kids." She set her book aside. "Their names are Nicholai and Natasha. Nick and Tasha."

"Who the fuck cares what their names are? I don't want to hear about them."

She looked at me levelly, then said, "You can't get up and walk out. So you're going to hear about them."

"I may have to hear. I don't have to listen."

Maddy ignored my petulance. "Their father was Ivan Kramer. Ukrainian. Their mother was Pina Roncarelli. Italian. She died giving birth to Tasha when Nick was four years old."

"So the kid says," I sneered.

"So the records at City Hall say. I thought you weren't listening."

"I'm a fucking captive audience. What the hell can I do but lie here and listen?"

"Poor Mikey," Maddy deadpanned. "Shall I go on?"

I scowled at her. She had piqued my curiosity and she knew it. This was the same person who had once told me bedtime stories. "Go ahead. I'm not going anywhere."

"Gotcha." Maddy grinned. "Okay. From here on, it's what Nick told me. What he remembers. When Pina died, Ivan brought in a cousin of hers to take care of the baby.

165

A young woman named Teresa. Terry. Nick thinks they got married, but there's no record Ivan ever made an honest woman of her. Ivan was killed in an accident on the construction site where he was working, and Terry, legal or not, ended up with the kids. Nick was six. Tasha was two."

Maddy's mouth tightened. "This is where it gets messy. Terry fell for a small-time hoodlum named Joey Lasalle. He moved in. And started abusing Nick. Physically and sexually. Then he included Tasha in his fun and games. He had that little girl sucking him off before she was four years old."

"Maddy! For God's sake!"

"Come on, Mike. You covered the courts. You have to know that sort of thing goes on."

"I know. I just don't like hearing expressions like that coming from you."

"You mean expressions like 'Hey, meestair, you wanna fuck my seestair?' "

"Okay. Okay. It was a stupid thing to say."

"It was more than stupid. By the time Tasha was six years old, that's exactly what Joey Lasalle was doing."

"Six years old? Where was the woman, what'sername, Terry? Where's Terry while all this is going on?"

"Out in space somewhere. One of Joey's little enterprises was drugs. Terry was his best customer."

"Uh. So the kid takes his sister and runs away."

"Not yet. You're getting ahead of me. What happened is, one day Nick heard Joey and a friend planning to rob a gas station. Nick listens, then calls the police and tells them what's going to happen. The police are waiting and Joey gets eighteen months. Except he's released after serving only nine months. He was getting out the day Nick came here."

"Why here? What the hell? Why me?"

"He thought you were rich and famous. Picture in the paper, on TV, you'd have to be rich and famous. And he'd saved your life. The papers said so. Actually, he didn't think of you until time ran out on him. Joey was coming home. That's when he grabbed his sister and ran."

"And he thinks I should take his sister."

"So do I. I think you should take both of them. Tasha and Nick."

"*What!*"

"Before you blow a fuse, listen to—"

"Goddammit, Maddy, have you lost your goddamn marbles?"

"—what I have to say." She rose from the chair and bent over me. Her voice was emotionless, the school principal speaking. "If I have to stuff a towel down your throat, I will. But you are going to listen."

I glared at her but kept my mouth shut. She was perfectly capable of carrying out her threat. Her face softened and she returned to her chair.

"You're the same age as Dad was when Mama died," she said. "Did you know that?"

I shook my head.

"It destroyed him. *Bozhu mi Bozhu, chomy?* That damn, dark Ukrainian thing. The tragic Slavic soul. He forgot about you, his son. Me. Everything but his own damn angst. He wallowed in it till the day he died."

Maddy leaned forward and touched my arm, her eyes misting. "I love you, Mikey," she said. "I love you more than anything in the world. And the thought of you becoming . . ." She shook her head. "It could happen. I can see it starting now."

"Maddy—"

"No." She brushed the dampness from her eyes with the heel of her hand. "Let me finish."

She took a tissue from her handbag, dabbed at her cheeks and delicately blew her nose. I waited. She wasn't an easy weeper and her tears affected me more than I would have admitted.

"I've done a lot of thinking." Her composure regained, she continued. "You'll be out of here in ten days. And you won't be able to manage alone. Not at first."

I felt a surge of consternation. "What? What do you mean? I assumed you would stay. I thought you'd—"

"No," she interrupted me firmly. "It wouldn't work. You'd bully me and I'd resent you. No. My life is there. I'm going back. Which means you'll need either a nurse or a housekeeper until you can get around on your own."

"I don't need a nurse. I don't want a housekeeper."

"Good," she said. "Because the way you've been behaving, they wouldn't last two days. But Nick would."

"Nick? The kid? Great. Exactly what I need. A twelve-year-old housekeeper."

"Why do you always have to be such a smart aleck? What you need is somebody to do your running around for you. And a cleaning woman once a week."

Maddy leaned forward, eyes suddenly glowing. "You should have seen Nick's face when he saw all your books. A kid in a candy store. Mikey, this boy is very, very bright. In all my years of teaching, I don't remember a child as quick and as sharp. It would be criminal for a young mind like that to be allowed to wither."

"Christ. The Missionary of Education rides again. Why does this sound so familiar to me?" I was losing ground and Maddy knew it. She zeroed in.

"Try it for three months. If it doesn't work, we'll make arrangements to find foster homes for them."

"Them? The girl too? Whoa. Maybe I could cope with the boy. But that little girl . . . I don't think so."

"Not Natasha. Not yet. She'll go to Villa Marie. It's a boarding school run by nuns."

"I know what the Villa Marie is. I also know it doesn't come free. You mind telling me how much sending a kid I don't even know to an overpriced school is going to cost me?"

"Not a penny. Villa Marie is on me." Maddy gathered her bag and her book into her arms. "It'll be part of the deal I make with Nick. I take care of his little sister. He takes care of my little brother."

Mike finished his beer and pushed the glass away. He eyed me askance.

"You said Nick thought watching me climb the stairs was funny," he said. "Did you notice whether he had his hands in his pockets?"

"As a matter of fact, he did. His back pockets."

Mike smiled. "When I got my prosthesis," he said, "Nick was all over me like a dirty shirt. He hovered. He mother-henned me to death. I couldn't take two steps without him grabbing me. He claimed he couldn't help it. His hands went out all by themselves. So I told him to keep his goddamn hands in his goddamn pockets."

Mike's smile faded. "That was a long time ago," he said. He glanced at his watch. "And we've been here too long. Nick could call anytime. We'd better get back to your place."

He picked up his cigarettes, pushed back his chair.

"Let's go," Mike said. "I'll tell you the rest on the way. . . ."

31

*. . . M*addy was right about one thing. The kid was smart.

I taught him to play chess. I needed an opponent. TV was crap and so were the new books. By Thanksgiving, I couldn't beat him. Same with cribbage. Same with backgammon. The only game I could take him in was Scrabble. Christ, words were my business. If he'd creamed me there, I'd have heaved him back into the street.

Maybe he'd started out using books as a retreat, but this twelve-year-old kid was the most omnivorous reader I've ever met. Totally indiscriminate. Anything from comic books to Shakespeare. He was like a billy goat. If it was on paper, he devoured it.

I was hopping around on crutches that fall. Cranky as a bear. He'd watch me, like a cornered animal watching its predator, ready to jump before it strikes.

I caught him in a few lies. He walked out on me a few times when I'm sure he wanted to beat my brains in. We were antagonists. Each with too much to lose to go that one step too far.

Maddy came up for Christmas. Natasha came home. The thing I remember most clearly about that first Christmas together was hearing Nick laugh. I had never heard him laugh before.

When the school term ended, Nick and Natasha went to Texas to stay with Maddy.

I wasn't prepared to miss the kid. I was stunned at how much I actually did miss him. My house is old, with creaks and groans in every aging joint. I was constantly looking up, expecting to see him. Nick and Meg had never met, but their ghosts roamed my big empty house together that summer.

A week before Labor Day, I went to pick the kids up at the airport. I watched Nick's head rising from the escalator well, black hair shaggy, green eyes searching. He caught sight of me and his face lit up like a summer sunrise. He had missed me too. I sent up thanks to the gods who occasionally reward the undeserving.

He started calling me Pop. I was Uncle Mike to Natasha. Maddy was Aunt Maddy. The Waltons we weren't. But the four of us, in a tenuous sort of way, became a family. Every holiday was reunion time.

Then Maddy died. We had spent the Easter break in Florida. A month later, she died in her sleep. I hadn't even known she had a bum heart. Typically Maddy. Go quietly, no fuss. And typically Maddy, she willed educational funds to both Natasha and Nick. College money.

Nick had just turned seventeen.

We'd never tried for the father-son bit. The kind of man my father was, I knew bugger all about being a father anyway. We were friends.

He was smart. He was so damn smart I'd forget he was a kid. We could talk all night. Argue if we didn't agree. He liked hearing about my years as a police reporter. At first he wanted to be a newspaperman. Then a cop. Then he figured the only winners in the system were the lawyers. That's what he decided to be. And he never changed his mind again.

I'll never forget the rush of pleasure I felt the first time I overheard my opinions and expressions coming out of his mouth. I guess I felt like any proud poppa would feel.

Hell, this was a kid any father would be proud of. He made the principal's honors list semester after semester. He was interscholastic wrestling champion. Track star. And one of the top tennis players in the high-school competitions.

He had a lot of friends. But no buddies. I don't recall a really close friend. The way young boys pal up together? He was basically a loner. He had a reputation for being laid back. Cool. That and his looks drove the girls crazy. You know the teenage drill. Mash notes. Giggling phone calls. He was expert at sidestepping them. He was too busy for more than casual friendships with girls. He thought they were too possessive, too demanding. And too silly. The only girl he made allowances for was Natasha.

Natasha.

Natasha found God. Which was fine. At first. She lost some of her shyness and learned to smile.

She'd come home for the weekend and insist Nick and I join in morning prayers. And evening prayers. That was okay, too. If it made her happy, what the hell? But by the time she was eleven, this kid was bucking for sainthood. Hours spent on her knees? Self-flagellation? What the hell kind of education was she getting?

She was very close to one of the nuns, Sister Carmela. A chunky young woman with a mustache and an irritating giggle. And to Father Paul, the parish priest, one of those sallow young ascetics with a caved-in chest and the eyes of a fanatic. She was his Virgin Mary in every Christmas pageant and a suffering saint in every damn religious tableau he ever staged.

I thought all the God bothering was unhealthy. Maddy said I was a benighted heathen, and sore because I had to watch my language when Natasha was home. She said lots of young girls go through a religious phase. Natasha would leave Villa Marie when she was thirteen and ready for high school. She would outgrow all the religious nonsense and all would be for the best in this best of all possible worlds.

Natasha was thirteen when Maddy died. Thirteen. With the face of Saint Joan and the body of Gina Lollobrigida.

On June thirteenth, she hung herself.

No warning. No note. One of the other students found her hanging in the stairwell.

Nick went deaf, dumb and blind. When I tried to talk to him, he looked at me as though he didn't know who I was. I made the necessary arrangements.

Nick and I were the only mourners. When the casket was lowered into the ground, he told me to go home alone. There was something he had to do. They were the first words he'd spoken since Natasha died.

I went home and waited. Waited and worried and waited. At two in the morning, I gave up and went to bed. I didn't expect to fall asleep, but I did.

When I wakened at seven, I knew he was home. I always knew when he was home. The house felt different.

I went down to the kitchen.

He was sitting at the kitchen table, hunched over the morning newspaper. Not reading. He was staring, white-faced and blank-eyed, at nothing.

"Nick? Where the hell have you—"

I stopped. He had shifted his gaze, and something in his empty eyes sent a chill through me. "Nick?"

He pushed the paper across the table.

In the lower right-hand section of the page was a single-column story headed "Parish Priest Beaten to Death."

I read the first paragraph—

> The body of Father Paul deVolpi was found last night in the parking lot at the rear of St. Veronica's Church. Police state that he was beaten to death by an unknown assailant.

"I didn't mean to kill him," Nick said, his voice a low monotone. "I went to beat the shit out of him. I didn't mean to kill him."

"Beat . . ." My good leg began trembling uncontrollably. I sat down. Hard. "Nick—"

"He raped her. He raped Tasha."

"Raped? Oh my God." The trembling had spread. I rubbed my face with a hand that shook. "How do you . . . who . . ."

"I went to see Sister Carmela at the convent. Right after the funeral."

"She . . . she told you that? She said . . ."

Nick's icy reserve finally cracked. He leaned forward, his eyes blazing green fire.

"You know Tasha, Pop. You know what her religion means . . . meant . . . to her. Suicide is a mortal sin. What could be worse, in her mind, than eternal damnation? I had to know, Pop. It was driving me crazy. I had to know why."

"They said . . . the Mother Superior said—"

"Fuck Mother Superior," Nick interrupted angrily. "Tasha wasn't depressed. Carmela tried to pull the same crap."

"Nick . . ." A sudden image of a battered Sister Carmela flashed through my mind.

"Come on, Pop. No. I didn't lay a hand on her. I didn't have to. She was scared shitless."

I nodded, remembering the thrill of fear Nick, then twelve years old, had once inspired in me.

"Tasha went to Sister Carmela. After." Nick's voice was suddenly hoarse. "You know what that cow said to her? What she told Tasha? She said Tasha had sinned. She had tempted Father Paul. *Tasha?* Jesus, Pop, Tasha was terrified of men. Even of you. To her, men meant brutal sex. Tasha tempted that sick bastard?"

"Easy, Nick." I reached across and placed a hand on his wrist. His hands were puffed, the skin on his knuckles broken and bloody. There was a dark stain on his shirt, another on the trousers of the suit he had worn to the funeral.

174

"Nick, did anyone see you? At Saint Veronica's? Did anyone see you there?"

"See me? I don't think so." Nick shook his head. "No. I don't think so. I waited in the parking lot. It was pretty dark. There's a high wall around the lot anyway. And Father Paul's was the only car. I don't think anybody saw me."

I stood up.

"Go get changed," I said. "Put something on those cuts on your hands. I'll make breakfast. We'll talk."

He was still young enough to look relieved that someone else was taking over.

"Bring those clothes you're wearing down with you," I called after him. "We'll get rid of them."

Twenty minutes later, he was back, showered and shaved, his knuckles stained now with iodine. He ate hungrily.

"Sister Carmela will tell the police about you," I said. "If she hasn't already."

He shook his head. "I don't think they'll even talk to her." He gestured toward the newspaper. "The paper says he was carrying parish money in a briefcase. He wasn't carrying anything when he came out of the church. They're covering up, making it look like a mugging. They don't want the kind of notoriety steering the police onto me would bring."

"You don't think Carmela will go to the police?"

"No. If she talks to anybody, it'll be to Father Paul's uncle. She'll go to Diano."

I set my cup down, startled. "Diano? Carmine Diano?"

Nick looked up from his eggs. "You know him?"

I nodded. "Do you know who he is?"

"I know who he is. Joey . . . Joey Lasalle . . . used to kiss his ass. I know who he is and what he is." Nick pushed his plate away, the eggs unfinished. "I've got to get going. I'll be late for school."

"You're going to school?"

"History exam." Nick stood up. He looked down at me, his eyes grave. "See you later, Pop. You'll be home?"

"Yeah. Sure. Take the car."

"Thanks, Pop."

He left. I sat and drank cold coffee.

Carmine Diano. By then, he wasn't small potatoes anymore. They were starting to refer to him as a crime kingpin, local godfather, all that Mafia crap. And this was a guy who took himself very, very seriously. There was no way his nephew was going to be dead without someone being hung out to dry.

If he accepted the police report, he'd find some two-bit hood, some junkie, anybody, and make a very nasty example of him. If Sister Carmela got to him, that somebody was going to be Nick.

Nick should have been home for lunch. Supper time came and went. No Nick. At ten o'clock, when I was thinking seriously of calling a police detective, a friend, and asking him to put out an alert on my car, in walked Nick. I blew.

He walked past me, into the kitchen, me yelling. He went to the fridge, brought out two beers. He brought them to the table and said, "Siddown, Pop."

I sat. I took a long swallow of beer, forced myself to cool down and said, "Goddamn it, Nick. Why the hell didn't you call? Where the hell have you been?"

"I went to see Diano."

I stared at him, speechless.

"I'm not going to spend the rest of my life looking over my shoulder to see if some Sicilian pimp is gaining on me."

My impulse to laugh at his choice of words was choked off by their toneless delivery. The total absence of emotion in a seventeen-year-old was chilling.

"Well," I said lamely, "you're still alive. So you must have done some pretty fast talking. What did he say?"

"He offered me a job."

"He . . . sure he did."

Nick smiled without humor. "He didn't exactly offer me a job. He told me I was going to work for him."

That smile alarmed me. "Or else?"

"Or else the tape he'd made of me confessing to the murder of Father Paul would be turned over to a friend. An associate of his. A police captain." Nick's smile faded. "Or he'd give me a choice between a meat hook and a pair of cement shoes."

32

$\mathcal{W}$e had reached home. Mike was silent as I made the turn into the driveway. I parked the car, turned off the motor.

"He went to work for Diano?" I asked. "At seventeen?"

"At seventeen. He rented an apartment in town that summer. He worked for Diano. In the fall, he entered law school."

"Maddy's money?"

Mike nodded. "For a while, we kept in touch. Then less and less. When he graduated, I went . . . but by then . . ." He broke off. Inside the house, the phone was ringing.

"Nick," he said.

Roxanne was replacing the phone in its cradle when we entered the kitchen.

"That was Charlie," she told us. Her eyes darted back and forth between Mike and me, trying to read our faces. "They're on their way back to town. They want to stop by to pick up the chest. They'll be here in five minutes."

Mike answered her unspoken question.

"He's going to help," he said. "He'll call here. We just have to wait."

A low moan escaped Roxanne. Steve moved to her.

"Hang in there, kid," he said gently. "You're doing fine." He circled her shoulders with his arm and turned to me. "So. Talk to us, Cat. You were gone a long time. What did Kramer have to say?"

"He told us we'd get a call from Liverlips . . . Vince. He said you'd get to speak to Cassie."

"She's still alive!" Roxanne's cry was ragged with emotion held in tight control. "That's what he means, isn't it? That she's still alive. Do you believe him? How would he know?"

"I'll tell you exactly what he said. And it made sense to me. He—" The doorbell rang. I went to answer it, calling back, "Mike, tell them what Nick said."

Charlie and Rafe were on the doorstep, Charlie, as always, looking larger than life.

"That was quick. Come on in."

"We weren't far away," Charlie said. "My chest ready?"

"Two coats. If you want three, I'll need another day."

Rafe smiled his oblique smile. "Why don't we take a look at it and see?"

They followed me to the kitchen. I introduced them to Mike.

"Mike Melnyk?" Charlie frowned. "Your face is familiar. Mike . . . Michael. Hey. The columnist. Didn't you used to be Michael Melnyk?"

"Still am," Mike said starchily.

"Aw, shit." Charlie was genuinely distressed. "I'm sorry, Mike. Excuse me all to hell. My mouth tends to work faster than my brain. But what in hell happened to you? You wrote a great column and suddenly—" Charlie stopped abruptly, then said quietly, "I remember now. Sorry, Mike. Life's a bitch sometimes, isn't it?"

Mike's gaze slid from Charlie's black eye patch to Rafe's scarred profile. "Sometimes it is," he nodded.

Rafe had been casually eyeing the photographs strewn on the table. He picked up one of the glossies.

"Charlie?" He held the photo out to Charlie. "Isn't this Lulu?"

"Lulu and Lala?" Charlie took the photo, inspected it. "Yeah, it's Lulu all right."

"Lulu?" I snatched the photo from Charlie. It was the shot of Liverlips and the Hulk. "What lulu?"

"Luigi Caruso and Larry Mendelsohn," Charlie said. "We make beautiful music together. Lulu and Lala."

I stared at him, dumbfounded. "Luigi? Lulu? That big ape is gay? Is that what you're saying?"

"Gay? No." Charlie's mouth curled. "Just a horny turd."

"You know him?" Mike asked. "You know Luigi?"

"Actually, we know Larry," Charlie said. "Sweet little guy. Does some picking for us. We've met Luigi a couple of times with Larry. At parties. Around. Why?"

Mike's eyes narrowed. "Do they live together?"

Charlie frowned. "I don't think so."

Steve and Mike exchanged glances.

"You thinking what I'm thinking?" Steve asked. "Vince could use a sweet little guy?"

Mike nodded. "He sure as hell couldn't take her home."

"Where does he live?" Steve turned to Charlie. "This guy Larry? Do you know where he lives?"

"Yeah. East End." Charlie frowned from one to the other. "Why all the interest?"

Rafe had been leaning against the wall, arms akimbo, head lowered, listening. He looked up at me.

"Cat? Where's Brandy? Where's the little girl? Cassie?"

The air stilled.

"Maybe if you told us what's going on, we could help." Rafe waited. Nobody moved. Nobody spoke. Then he added in a quiet voice, "That's what friends are for, Cat."

I related an abridged version of the events of the past two weeks, a story that was becoming increasingly bizarre to my own ears. Other than exchanging a startled glance at the bank episode, they listened without comment until I finished.

"Never did like that Luigi bastard," Charlie growled. He looked at Rafe. "You think maybe we can call Larry and feel him out?"

"No," Mike intervened sharply. "Start asking questions and they'll get the wind up."

"You don't know Larry," Charlie smiled. "Ask Larry how he is, you get a blow-by-blow, you should excuse the expression, account of his life and times. In minute detail. Including his sex life and his bowel movements."

"We can't call him," Rafe said. "He has an unlisted number since that mess with Harry. You drove him home once, Charlie. Where does he live?"

"One of those dinky apartments above Nathan's Book Store. On Hutchison. He baby-sits the store for Nate occasionally."

"Would Nate have the unlisted number?"

"Why don't we find out?" As Charlie crossed to the phone, he drew a small black book from his jacket pocket. He thumbed through it, then dialed, talking over his shoulder.

"This could take a couple of minutes. Nate's a talker. He's in a wheelchair and he lives behind the store. So he tends to—" Charlie interrupted himself. "Nate? It's Charlie. Charlie Harwood. How's it going?"

Charlie listened. "Nate . . ." he began, then listened, his one eye raised, fingers drumming the countertop.

"Nate!" he shouted finally. "Nate? We're trying to get in touch with Larry. Do you have his number? The unlisted one?" He listened, grimaced, shook his head at Rafe. "Nate? If you happen to see him—" He stopped, his expression sharpening. "He did? Okay! Thanks, Nate."

Charlie hung up and slapped his hand on the counter. He exhaled a triumphant "Yes!"

"He was in Nate's a couple of hours ago. He bought a kid's book for his niece. Except Larry doesn't have a niece. The only family he has are his grandparents. And them he hates."

"Where on Hutchison?" Steve was halfway across the room, Roxanne at his heels.

"We're going with you," Charlie said. "If Larry's alone, he'll let us in. If Luigi's there, you'll need help."

Steve halted. "You sure?" he asked dubiously. "Things could get rough."

Charlie grinned. "Hey, I'm not as fragile as I look," he said. "And Rafe fights dirty."

"Okay. Thanks, Charlie." Steve turned to Mike. "I think you and Cat should wait here for Nick's call, Mike. This thing with Larry sounds right, but who knows? Let's cover all the bases. If it turns out to be a dud and Nick comes up with something, you'll need Cat with you. Cassie doesn't know you."

Mike nodded. "Makes sense. Good luck."

I raised a pair of crossed fingers to Roxanne. She smiled tremulously and the four of them hurried out. We heard Rafe's van start up, then the squeal of tires as it raced down the driveway.

"Nice people," Mike said. "What's the story there?"

"Rafe's face? Charlie's eye?" I stood up. "I'm going to make coffee. Are you hungry?"

Mike shook his head. "Coffee sounds good, though."

The coffee had just begun to perk and I was barely into the meeting between Charlie and Rafe when the phone rang. Mike jumped to answer.

"Hello?" He nodded to me, mouthed *Nick* and listened intently. "I know where it is," he said. He nodded, said, "Okay," and hung up. "Let's go, Cat."

"What did he say? Does he know where—"

Mike was halfway down the hall, moving faster than I would have thought possible. "I'll tell you on the way," he called back. "Come on."

I grabbed my purse and keys and hurried after him.

"Do you know where Canal Street is?" he asked as we ran to the car.

"No."

"Gimme the keys. I'll drive."

The way he peeled out the driveway should have warned me. He drove as though the car was an adversary to be beaten into submission. At the first corner, he barely touched the brake. He shot through a yellow light, tramping on the accelerator.

"It's not far," he said. "Canal's just off Lakeshore."

I pressed both feet against the fire wall, clenched my fists in my lap. "What did Nick say?"

"He's at MoCan. Vince. Got there about half an hour ago."

"What's—"

Mike trod on the brake as the traffic light turned red. Instinctively, I flung both hands to the dashboard. Without the seat belt, my arms would have snapped like twigs. Or I'd have hurtled through the windshield.

"What's Mocan?" I asked shakily.

"MoCan. Mobile Cantine. It's one of the companies Vince controls. He told the night manager to take off. He'd close up. Nick must have put out the word. The manager called Nick when he got home. He'll meet us there. Nick."

The light changed and we leaped forward. I kept my hands braced on the dash and closed my eyes.

"According to the manager, he's never pulled this before. Vince. Never closed up the place. Nick says there's no reason for Vince to be there."

Mike was silent. I opened my eyes, closed them again as he crossed lanes, cutting off a black van. I heard the bleating of an angry horn fade behind us, felt the car swerve into a right turn and decrease speed.

I opened my eyes.

We were on an industrial boulevard, dimly lit, with streetlights every second block. Our headlights picked up the red gleam of taillights on trucks parked against dark buildings looming on each side of the road. There was no traffic between us and the lake, glinting under the moon several blocks down. We were the only car moving.

Halfway down, Mike killed the headlights and made a sharp U turn. He drifted to a stop beside a high chain fence and turned off the motor.

"This is it." He reached for the door latch. "When you get out, don't slam the door."

"Aren't we going to wait for Nick?"

"We can wait up there." He gestured with his head. "I want to make sure Vince is still around."

I was trying to latch the car door silently when I heard a loud thump on the hood of the car. My heart leaped into my throat.

"*The lighthouses!*" The words came out in a loud whisper. Mike stood across from me, his fist on the hood of the car, his eyes gleaming in the reflected light of the pale moon. "The goddamn lighthouses!"

"What are you talking about?"

He leaned on the hood of the car.

"What was the first thing Carmine said to you? What did he say when we walked into that office?"

I thought back. "Something about the bank robber who saved his life?"

"He said, '*so this is the beautiful bank robber who saved my life,*'" Mike corrected.

"Okay. So?"

"So it's been bugging me all night. *How did Carmine know about the bank robbery?*"

"I told . . ."

"You told *Nick*. Down in the dining room. And by the time we get upstairs Carmine knows all about the bank? Come on, Cat."

He was right. I'd missed it entirely. "So how . . . ?"

"The lighthouse. It's a microphone. Nick has your whole story on tape."

"Nick?"

"Who else? The Capri is his. Jesus, what an edge. The place is practically a private club for organized crime honchos and he has it wired for sound. A lighthouse on every table. And I'll bet my good leg there's a monitor behind that fancy screen in his office." Mike limped around the car. "Come on. Let's go see if Vince's car is still here."

The MoCan building was situated farther back from the street than its neighbors and was approached by a narrow road, barely wide enough for two cars to pass. It was a corridor, perhaps a hundred yards long, walled on each side by a high, wire-mesh fence behind which were parked silvery mobile cantines, one beside the other, ranged like snub-nosed, black-visored guards from a Star Wars movie.

We could see the dark bulk of the building at the end of the corridor. Mike pointed silently to a lighted window in the otherwise dark second story.

The corridor ended when the wire-mesh fences took sudden right-angle turns, creating a large parking quadrangle in front of the yellow brick structure. Vince's Jaguar, gleaming in spotlights aimed from a cantilevered canopy, was parked in front of the concrete steps rising to the entrance doors.

"Okay. He's here," I whispered. "Do we stay here, or do we go back to the car and wait for Nick?"

"We're here. We might as well wait here."

"What if he comes out before Nick gets here?"

"Let's go over there." Mike pointed to what appeared to be lumber piled against a loading platform a few feet to the right of the entrance.

We crossed the quadrangle, watchful for any telltale silhouette in the lighted window above.

The lumber turned out to be a six-foot-high stack of wooden shipping pallets. Someone had been at work constructing them. Two-by-twos, uniform in length, leaned along the building; two-by-sixes lay piled against the loading platform.

Mike prowled around the pallets and disappeared. I kept my eye on the road. Where was Kramer?

"*Cat.*" The hiss came from behind the lumber.

The pallets had been stacked a short distance from the wall of the building, creating a narrow tunnel approximately three feet wide by six feet long.

"We'll wait in there," Mike whispered. He gestured for me to enter the darkened tunnel, then followed me in. "We can see everything from here."

The two-inch-deep spaces between the stacked pallets were like gun slits in a bunker. We could see the long corridor to the street and a fair section of the street itself. The view of the quadrangle was blocked off. Liverlips' car and the entrance to the building were visible through the open end of our tunnel.

We had barely settled in when a car turned in from the street, its headlights glancing off the rows of sentinel vans, illuminating the long corridor leading to where we waited. I moved against Mike, expecting him to step out of our hiding place.

"Wait," he hissed. He reached for a two-by-two from the wall. "We can't see who's in the car. Wait till he parks."

We lost sight of the car when it reached the quadrangle, then found it again as it rolled into view on our right. It came to a halt, parked directly behind Vince's Jag.

The headlights snapped off. The door on the driver's side swung wide. Luigi Caruso stepped out.

I felt Mike stiffen. My heart was beating in my throat as we watched Luigi circle the rear of the car. He opened the door on the passenger's side and bent into the front seat. When he straightened, he had Cassie, a limp rag doll, in his arms. Without bothering to close the door, he turned and headed for the concrete steps leading up to the entrance doors of the building.

Mike was gone before I had absorbed what I was seeing. Running crookedly, he covered the ground between us and the stairs with amazing speed, reaching the bottom of the stairs as Luigi prepared to mount the second step. He swung the two-by-two wide behind him and brought it around, catching Luigi behind the knee of the leg on which he was balanced.

"Cat!" Mike shouted. "Get Cassie! *Run!*"

Luigi fell back heavily, landing sprawled at the bottom of the stairs, still holding Cassie. As I raced out to get her, Mike raised the two-by-two high above his head and brought it down with full force on Luigi's kneecap.

Luigi let out a bellow of rage and pain. He was scrabbling backwards, away from Mike, as I snatched Cassie from him. He reared up, struck his head on the door he had left open and howled again. Mike raised the two-by-two above his head once more.

I turned and ran, carrying Cassie's deadweight awkwardly. I was across the quadrangle and well into the corridor before I looked back.

Mike had reached the beginning of the corridor. Behind him, the entrance doors to the building flew open and Vince ran out onto the concrete platform. He hesitated, then raced to his car.

My heart plummeted.

He's going to run us down. I can't run any faster. Too many years of cigarettes. Too many years of no exercise. Too many years. Oh God, I'm too old for this.

There was a thunderous thump and roar. The quadrangle turned a brilliant white. Every detail of what I saw etched itself vividly before I dropped to the ground. I saw Mike fall, barely into the corridor. The quadrangle turned a lurid red as flames mounted to the sky from the spot the Jag had occupied.

I had dropped Cassie. As I knelt to pick her up, headlights swept into the corridor. The chrome grille of a car stopped feet from where I crouched. The passenger door swung open and Carmine Diano stepped out.

187

The sight of him filled me with a sudden searing rage. I leaped to my feet and ran at him, screaming.

"You bastard! You lying bastard! Cassie could have been in that car! You've killed Mike! You lied! You lied! You dirty whoremonger!"

Carmine's face, yellow in the reflection of the flames behind me, turned savage. He raised his arm and swept it in a backhanded arc, smashing into my right cheek with his closed fist. My head exploded. I dropped to my knees at his feet.

"Gino!" The word cracked above me like a whip.

I raised my head. Nick Kramer stood between me and Diano. Gino, the man with the El Greco eyes, emerged from behind the wheel of the car. Behind him were the headlights of a second car, left with its motor running.

"Take my car." Nick's voice was icy. "Get him out of here. Throw me your keys."

"They're in the car, Nick."

"Then get going." He swung on Diano. "You'd better get out of here, Carmine. Fast."

Gino and Diano turned and ran. Seconds later, the rear car shot backward out of the corridor and spun, tires screaming, into the street.

Nick reached down for my arm and yanked me to my feet.

"Get the kid in the car. I'm going after Mike."

I picked Cassie up and held her face against my cheek. Her soft breath stirred my hair. She was alive. I laid her gently on the rear seat of the car, then ran to follow Nick.

He had Mike's left arm across his shoulders and was trying to raise him to his feet. Mike's right arm hung limply. His legs were crossed, the prosthesis on his left leg twisted at a crazy angle around his right leg.

As I bent and separated the two, Mike grunted out two words. "I'm . . . o . . . kay."

I stood up, grasped him around his waist and together, Nick and I pulled him to his feet.

"Let's go," Nick said, and we ran, clumsily, half carrying, half dragging, Mike between us.

"Just . . . had the . . . breath knocked . . ." Mike panted.

"Shut up, Mike," Nick snapped. "Save your breath. The place will be crawling with cops any second. Just concentrate on getting out of here."

We reached the car and unloaded Mike into the passenger seat. I climbed into the back of the car next to Cassie, barely slamming the door before we were speeding in reverse out to the street. Nick brought the car to a halt beside my car. He leaped from the driver's seat and ran around to help Mike from the car.

"Okay, I'm okay," Mike grunted. "Get the kid."

Nick moved Cassie into the backseat of my car while Mike hobbled around the hood. He settled into the passenger seat, lifted his left leg into the car with both hands and swung his right leg in beside it. I got behind the wheel.

Nick closed the rear door and bent down to the open window beside me.

"Get out of here," he said. He slapped the side of the car and stepped back.

"Wait! Nick!" Mike leaned across me. "I want the tape."

Nick went still, his face expressionless.

"I gotta tell you, Nick," Mike grinned up at him, "those lighthouses of yours are tacky. Really tacky."

Nick's eyes glinted green, then he laughed.

"Tomorrow," he said. "You'll have it tomorrow."

"No copies?"

"No copies. Now get the hell out of here."

By the time I found my keys and started the motor, Nick's car was a pair of red eyes winking in the distance.

Mike rummaged, grumbling, through his pockets, found

his cigarettes and pressed the dashboard lighter. "Cassie?" he asked, waiting. "She okay?"

"I think so. She's breathing. I think she's been drugged."

"You want a cigarette?"

"Not right now." I turned my aching head, shook it and instantly regretted it. "Thanks anyway."

"What the hell happened to you?" Mike bent toward me. He touched my cheek. I winced and he withdrew his hand.

"Diano socked me."

"Diano? Carmine was there? When? I didn't see him."

"Only for a minute or two. Nick told that man, Gino, to get him out of there."

"What did he hit you for?"

"Probably because I called him a lying whoremonger."

"Whoremonger? You called Diano a whoremonger?" Mike began to chuckle. He pointed ahead. "Turn right at the corner, Cat. Let's get off this street."

I made the turn. Halfway down the block, a police car sped past us, dome light flashing red, siren wailing.

33

There was only one vehicle parked in the driveway: Steve's van. They weren't back yet. I pulled up beside it and handed the keys to Mike.

"Can you make it to the front door?"

Mike nodded. "I think so."

"It's the brass key. I'll get Cassie."

Mike hopped and limped around the car and up the steps. He unlocked the front door and held it open for me. I carried Cassie straight to her bedroom, stripped her, pulled a clean nightgown over her head and tucked her into bed.

Her face was pale and there were dark circles under her eyes, but she was breathing evenly, naturally. I brushed the hair from her face, bent and kissed her warm cheek, reached to turn off the light, then decided to leave it on. I went to the bathroom and looked at myself in the mirror.

The right side of my face was swollen from above my eye down to my jaw; my cheekbone was lost under a mottled purple bruise. My eye was almost closed, the upper lid tight and glossy. I was going to have one hell of a black eye.

I wrung a towel out in cold water and pressed it against my throbbing cheek, closing my eyes against the sudden shock of pain. Behind my eyelids, Vince's car exploded once again. I opened my eyes and stared at myself.

I had witnessed the incineration of a human being. Perhaps two. And my only thought was: *I hope my clothes—the dress, the wig, the shoes, the yellow bag—were in Vince's trunk when it burned.*

Mike had helped himself to the coffee I had set to perk a lifetime ago. He sat at the kitchen table, leaning on his elbows, sucking in smoke.

"That has to be battery acid by now," I said. "How can you drink it?"

He shrugged. "It's coffee. I've had worse."

"I'll make fresh." I dumped the stale coffee in the sink and filled the percolater with fresh water. "Shouldn't they be back by now?"

"They had a lot farther to go than we did."

"Mike?" I rinsed the used coffee grounds out of the perk top and replaced them with fresh. "Does it bother you they're dead? Vince and Luigi? The way they died?"

"No." He hesitated, then said more positively, "No, it doesn't. Is it bothering you? Don't let it, Cat. Believe me, they were garbage. Both of them."

"Do you think Luigi may have survived?"

Mike shook his head. "He was almost directly under the trunk of Vince's car when it blew. There is absolutely no way he could have survived."

"Who wired the car? Do you think Nick—"

"Not Nick. Carmine. He couldn't care less about Cassie. He had the car wired and he came to make bloody sure Vince went up with it." He tilted his head. "Do you hear a car?"

It was Rafe's van. Roxanne, pale and drawn, stepped down from the passenger's seat. Her eyes widened when she saw my face. I cut her off before she could speak.

"She's home. We got her. She's home. Safe. In bed."

Roxanne raced past me.

"She's been drugged," I called after her. "We *think* she was drugged."

"She was." Charlie slid the van door back and climbed out. "We know."

"How? How do you know?"

"First things first." He leaned into the van. "Hand him out, Steve."

Steve appeared in the van doorway, supporting a slender man who had been savagely beaten. His blond hair was crusty with dried blood. There was blood on his face, on his shirt, on his hands. One eye was completely closed. His lips were split and swollen, the color of raw steak. He was bent, his shoulders hunched as though each breath was agony, his left hand tucked under his right armpit. Charlie reached up and gently lowered him to the ground.

"Take it easy, kid," Charlie said softly. "Cat, this is Larry Mendelsohn."

"Larry Mendelsohn? Good God. What happened to him? Why didn't you take him to a hospital?"

"He wouldn't go. And we couldn't leave him alone. Luigi might have come back. So . . ." Charlie shrugged.

"Luigi did this?" I winced as Larry's leg buckled under him. "Bring him in the house. And you can forget Luigi." I felt a surge of malevolent satisfaction. "Luigi's dead."

Larry's good eye widened, fastened on me. His puffed lips parted. Before he or the other three could speak, I snapped, "First things first. Get him into the house."

They took him to the kitchen. I went to the bathroom for my first-aid kit and clean towels. When I entered the kitchen, Steve was at the phone, bent over the open phone book.

"I'm ordering pizza, Cat," he said. "We're all starving. Which of these—" He looked up. "Jesus Christ! What the hell happened to you?"

"I walked into a door." I set the first-aid kit on the table where Larry was seated and went to the sink for a bowl and warm water. "Wait till Roxanne comes out. You'll get the whole story. Tell us what happened with you. Why did Luigi do this to Larry? Begin at the beginning."

After several conflicting starts by Charlie and Steve, it was Rafe, finally, who was elected to tell their story.

Steve phoned for pizza, then perched on the counter with a mug of coffee in his hands. Charlie took the chair opposite Larry and held his hand while I went to work cleaning him up. Mike sat back, smoking and listening.

"Luigi told Larry that Cassie was the daughter of a friend of his," Rafe began. "A woman who had to go into the hospital overnight for some tests. Evidently everything went fine until after supper. Larry read to Cassie, the books he had bought from Nate. They watched TV for a while. Then Cassie started to cry. She wouldn't stop and Luigi blew. He told Larry to shut her up or he'd do it himself."

"I told Lulu . . ." Larry's words were distorted by his grotesque lips.

"Don't talk," I said firmly. "Wait till I'm finished."

The damage wasn't as bad as it looked. Most of the blood was from a cut in his forehead—a vein had bled profusely—and his battered nose. The cut wasn't deep enough to require stitches and his nose would heal. His left hand had swelled to double the size of his right, but he was able to wiggle his fingers. I bound his hand with an elastic bandage.

"Cassie wouldn't stop crying and Luigi got out a needle. So Larry took Cassie into the bathroom and locked the door. Luigi broke down the door. Larry tried to get past him with Cassie. That's when Luigi started beating on him. Larry said he lost consciousness for a few minutes. When he came to, Luigi was on the phone and Cassie was out cold. Luigi hung up, grabbed Cassie and headed for the door. Larry went after him. Luigi knocked him out again. When Larry regained consciousness this time, they were gone. That's when we arrived."

"Is Cassie all right?" Larry's words through swollen lips were mangled and his blue eyes appealed to me for reassurance. "I really tried—"

"She's all right. You did everything you could. Now don't worry. She's fine."

There was something artlessly appealing about him. His unmarked eye was guileless, almond-shaped, tilted and large. His blond hair had the silky texture of a child's. His skull had felt delicate under my fingers, in the way the fragile bones of a bird feel beneath their protective layers of down and feathers.

"Relax, Larry. You done good, kid." Charlie reached over and gently touched Larry's battered face. "Think you'll be able to manage pizza?"

Larry shook his head. "My mouth hurts too much. I think my teeth are loose." He was barely understandable.

"Are you hungry?"

Larry nodded. He looked at Charlie mournfully.

Charlie stood up. "Got any bananas, Cat?" he asked briskly. "Eggs? Milk? Blender?"

"Blender's in the cupboard above the stove. Bananas are there." I pointed to the fruit bowl on the dishwasher. "Eggs and milk in the fridge."

Rafe winked at me as Charlie bustled about, berating Larry as he moved from fridge to counter.

"What the hell's the matter with you, Larry? You have some kind of death wish or something? When are you going to stop getting yourself involved with arseholes like Luigi? What the hell did you see in that revolting bastard anyway?"

"He said he loved me." The words were wistful.

"Aw, for Christ's sake." Charlie cracked an egg force-fully into the blender. "So did Harry. And he broke your fucking arm. And that creep, Phil? The sonovabitch took off with your sound system and your CD's. And that sleazy lawyer, what was his name, the one who had you donating your ass to all his closet clients? One of whom, if I remember correctly, broke your fucking nose."

Charlie splashed milk into the container, peeled a banana

and added it to the milk and egg. He threw the blender switch and roared over the buzz, "Christ Almighty, Larry, if losing your pretty face doesn't scare you, doesn't AIDS?"

Larry's head drooped on his slender neck. "I'm not lucky, Charlie," he said meekly. "I'm just not lucky."

"Luck has nothing to do with it, you silly bitch," Charlie snapped. He turned to me. "Got any straws, Cat?"

"Drawer next to the dishwasher. Glasses above the sink."

Charlie scavenged in the drawer, reached in the cupboard above the sink. He poured the foaming liquid from the blender into a glass, stabbed a straw into it and brought it to the table. "Here. Sip this."

He stationed himself, arms akimbo, above Larry, glowering down at him. "Larry, you have to break this self-destructive pattern of yours before some perverted sonovabitch maims you for life. And don't kid yourself it can't happen to you. Ask Rafe. Tell him, Rafe. Maybe you can talk some sense into this poor misguided twit."

Rafe's brows lifted. "*Me?* No way. You're doing just fine." The doorbell rang and he leaped to his feet. "The pizza. I'll get it."

Steve dropped from the counter. "I'll get it, Rafe."

"I'll get it," Rafe insisted, halfway out of the kitchen. "You go get Roxanne."

I glanced at Mike. He was contemplating Charlie, his chin propped in his hand, a small smile on his face. He caught my eye and his shoulders lifted an inch or two in a gentle shrug of amusement.

"Come on, baby." Charlie brushed hair back from the blue-black bruise on Larry's forehead. "Drink your dinner."

Rafe returned, carrying the familiar flat cardboard box. He set it on the counter and opened one end to slide the pizza out.

"How many of us?" He turned, raised one finger to

count noses and suddenly burst into laughter—rusty, throaty sounds of mirth that increased as he looked from one to the other of our confused faces.

"Hey. What's so damn funny?" Charlie scowled at him.

"Funny? We are." Rafe's laughter diminished to a chuckle. "Look at us. A one-eyed fruitcake who thinks he's Mother Teresa. A one-legged superannuated Don Quixote. Look at Larry. A one-hundred-and-ten-pound chicken with a mouth like a Ubangi. And Cat, a larcenous lady with a shiner you could use to light a city block. Me with a face that makes grown men cross themselves. It would take all five of us to put together one normal human being."

Mike grinned his clown's grin, shoulders shaking with silent laughter. Charlie, his golden eye glinting, chortled gleefully. Even Larry, his taped hand pressed to his battered mouth, emitted squeaks and snuffles of laughter. I held my throbbing cheek and tried not to smile too broadly.

"What's funny?"

Steve appeared in the doorway, Roxanne behind him. He eyed us, one after the other, a quizzical expression on his face. "What's so funny?"

"Rafe said . . ." Charlie began, then waved away an explanation with a flapping palm. "Forget it. You had to be here. Let's eat the pizza while it's still warm. Roxanne, cut it in six. I'll get plates. Cat? Got any paper napkins?"

"Paper towels." I pointed to the roll beside the sink and was abruptly overwhelmed by a monstrous wave of fatigue. My leaden arm fell to my lap.

"Roxanne's here." Charlie methodically tore off six sheets of toweling. "So, Cat, tell us what happened."

"I'm sorry." I pushed myself up from the table. My head pounded. I was emotionally drained and physically exhausted. "Mike will tell you. I'm sorry. I have to go to bed. Right now. Please excuse me."

I tottered down the hall, one hand braced against the

wall. Someone had yanked out my spine. Someone else had added half a mile to the length of the hall.

"Cat? Are you all right?" Roxanne's voice behind me was anxious.

"I'm okay. I'm fine. I'm dead."

I veered right, into my bedroom. I didn't brush my teeth. I didn't wash my face. I stepped out of my clothes, left them in a puddle on the floor and slid into my unmade bed, moaning with gratitude for its familiar comfort, for cool sheets.

Seconds later, a cold, damp cloth was placed gently over my eyes, a soft kiss touched my cheek.

"Good night, Cat," Roxanne said softly.

Behind my eyelids, Vince's car exploded. Flames bloomed and mounted to a black sky, dimming the stars.

Then I fell off the edge of the world.

34

"Wake up, Cat. Cat? Wake up."

I was instantly awake from a dream in which I was racing ahead of a molten lava stream pouring downhill, threatening to engulf me. I sat bolt upright, my heart pounding. "What? What?"

Roxanne drew back, startled. "Mort's on the phone and says he has to talk to you. He sounds mad. I mean mad big-time."

The jangling inside my head subsided to a plodding pulse beat. "What time is it?"

"Just after ten." Roxanne picked up my housecoat from the floor and held it for me. "I didn't want to wake you. But he said he'd keep calling till he got you." She followed me down the hall to the kitchen. "He's called four times so far."

I picked up the phone. "Hello?"

"Catherine? You gotta call them." It was Mort all right. The rasping voice drilling into my ear made me wince. He sounded angry. But Mort always sounded angry. "Tell them I did what they said. Call them now."

"What?" My head was filled with wet cement. I understood the words but couldn't put them together to make sense.

"I put my brother on the plane an hour ago. Just like they said." There was more than anger in his voice. There was fear. "He'll be there before noon. You'll have it before noon. I swear on the heads of my kids. Call them. Tell them."

"Call them? Call who?"

The line was silent for a second. Then Mort, his voice deadened, said, "Okay, Catherine. That's the way you want to play it, okay. But I did what they said. Exactly what they said. You tell them that. You call them. You tell them."

He hung up. I looked at the phone in astonishment.

"What?" Roxanne frowned.

"I don't know." I shook my head. "Didn't make any sense." I replaced the phone in its cradle. "Where's Cassie? Is she all right?"

"She's fine." Roxanne moved to the door and looked out at the patio, her arms folded across her breasts. "A bit subdued, but she's all right." She turned to me, her face distressed. "She misses Brandy. I haven't told her . . . I don't know what to tell her."

"I'll get dressed." Missing Brandy, that's still to come. "We'll try the Canis Major bit. It worked with Laurie."

"The what?"

"Canis Major. Sirius. The dog star. It's the brightest star in the heavens. I told Laurie that Tippy was in heaven. That she could see him in the sky every night."

"That worked?"

"That and a new puppy."

Roxanne grinned. "Go get dressed. I'll make a pot of fresh coffee."

The doorbell shrilled as I went down the hall. I detoured to the front door.

Nick Kramer stood on the flagstone stoop, a long florist's box under one arm, a stuffed toy dog under the other, a black leather briefcase dangling from his left hand.

"Good morning, Catherine." He smiled his white smile.

The toy dog wriggled, a pink tongue appeared. A puppy. A white, fluffy ball of live puppy.

"May I come in?"

"I'm sorry." I pushed the screen door open. "Of course. Please. Come in."

He stepped into the hall just as Roxanne emerged from the kitchen, her face questioning.

"Nick. Roxanne." I gestured an introduction. "Look. Give me a minute. I'll get dressed. Roxanne, maybe Nick would like a cup of coffee."

"Of course." Roxanne smiled and took the squirming puppy from under Nick's arm. He followed her to the kitchen.

I changed hastily into jeans and shirt. In the bathroom, I inspected my cheek, gingerly pressed a damp cloth against the black, blue and yellow bruises. I brushed my teeth, swallowed an aspirin and ran a comb through my hair. I looked faintly disreputable but I felt better.

Nick rose to his feet as I entered the kitchen, surprising me. I wondered if Mike had taught him the niceties.

Cassie was sprawled on the floor, nose to nose with the puppy.

"Look, Auntie Cat," she cried, her face alight. The puppy licked her flushed cheek, crouched down on its forelegs and waved a fluffy stump of tail. "Look. She likes me."

"What's her name? Does she have a name?"

"Sasha," Nick said. He glanced rather pointedly at his watch. "Her name is Sasha."

Roxanne had caught the look.

"Cassie? Why don't we take Sasha outside and let her run?" she suggested. "You can throw your ball for her."

Cassie bounded out the door, Sasha at her heels. Roxanne followed. "There's fresh coffee," she said and let the screen door close behind her.

I poured coffee for myself, raised the pot inquiringly at Nick. He shook his head, gestured at the florist's box.

"The flowers are from Carmine," he said.

I pulled off the light-gray cardboard lid and folded back the green waxy paper. Long-stemmed red roses. At least two dozen, lying on fronds of fragile green fern. I wrinkled my nose at them.

"You don't like them?" Nick sounded amused.

"If they're meant as an apology, he wasted his money." I pushed the flowers aside, took my cup and sat down opposite Nick. "What about Sasha? From Carmine, too."

"No. From me. She's three months old. She's had her shots. And she's been spayed." He reached into his brief-case, withdrew a black cassette and slid it across the table. "The tape," he said. "As promised."

I looked down at the cassette and something stirred in the back of my mind, made a connection.

"Mort Snyder. I told you about him." I tapped the cassette. "You got his name from the tape."

Nick said nothing, his face gave nothing away. He waited.

"Mort called this morning." I leaned forward. "He was mad and he was scared. Did you talk to him?"

"Not personally. No."

"Not personally." I felt a sudden chill. "I see. He said I'd have it this morning. What is it I'll have?"

"If it isn't your sixty thousand—" the green eyes smiled behind their screen of black lashes "—and a release on your house, Mort is going to have a very unhappy day."

"Oh." I had a vision of men with hard faces visiting Mort. For a brief, very brief, moment I felt a tug of sympathy for him. "Thank you," I said.

"No problem." Nick snapped his briefcase closed and rose to his feet. I followed him to the front door. He opened the door, hesitated.

"Is Mike all right?" he asked softly.

"Yes. He is. Why don't you call him?"

Nick looked at me, smiled. "Goodbye, Catherine."

"Goodbye, Nick."

I watched him stride to his car, a long, low, cream sports model. It started with a powerful growl and wheeled off down the driveway, turned into the street and sped out of sight.

I returned to the kitchen, poured coffee for myself and for Roxanne and carried the cups out to the rear patio. Roxanne saw me. She left Cassie and Sasha frolicking in the grass, came and dropped into the chaise beside me.

"He's gone?"

I nodded. "What did you think of him?"

She sipped her coffee thoughtfully. "Drop-dead gorgeous," she said at last. "But scary. Very scary. Flowers and puppy notwithstanding. Did he bring the tape?"

I nodded, then told her about Mort. She laughed gleefully.

"They made him an offer he couldn't refuse," she chortled. "I love it. I love it. Oh, Cat, it's over. You're okay, we're okay, and it's finally, finally over!"

Mort's certified check arrived at twelve-thirty. Sixty thousand dollars. My sixty thousand dollars. And a notarized quittance on my house. We piled into the car, Cassie and Sasha in the rear seat. I deposited the check, visited my safety deposit box and we returned home.

Steve was waiting for us. He scooped up Cassie and Sasha, kissed Roxanne and made a rude remark about my black eye.

While Roxanne prepared lunch, she brought him up to date. I searched for a cardboard box, found one the right size and packed the thirty-five thousand from my safety deposit box.

Brown paper. Felt-tipped pen. I printed, using my left hand.

I DIDN'T NEED IT AFTER ALL. THANK YOU.

I placed the note in with the money. I wrapped the box in brown paper. I printed "Manager—Urgent" in large black letters on the package. Then I sat and frowned at it.

Roxanne glanced over. "What's the matter?"

"The box is too big for the night-deposit slot."

"So?"

"So I've got a problem. Taking the money was easy. How do I give it back without being caught?"